FENELLA J. MILLER

THE RECLUSIVE DUKE

Complete and Unabridged

LINFORD
Leicester

First published in Great Britain in 2017

First Linford Edition
published 2018

A catalogue record for this book is available
from the British Library.

ISBN 978–1–4448–3618–9

Published by
F. A. Thorpe (Publishing)
Anstey, Leicestershire

Set by Words & Graphics Ltd.
Anstey, Leicestershire
Printed and bound in Great Britain by
T. J. International Ltd., Padstow, Cornwall

This book is printed on acid-free paper

1

'I'm damned if I will,' Everett said, and threw the document he was perusing into the fire.

'Your grace, I implore you, reconsider; you have ample room at Hemingford for a dozen children.' Mr Digby wrung his hands as he watched the letter burn. 'Hemingford Court is so vast you will scarcely know four children, their governess and the nursemaids are in residence.'

'If I wanted a parcel of brats here, I would set up my own nursery. My God, man, their relationship to me is so tenuous as to be almost non-existent. There must be someone else they can go to. I'll not have them here.' He glared at his lawyer, who got the message. 'I pay you to take care of things for me — take care of this. I don't wish to hear about it again.'

'Very well, your grace, I shall do as you bid. I take it you are prepared to provide the necessary financial support for the children even if they cannot reside here?'

'I have deep pockets, so you may set up an account and administer it as you see fit.'

His lawyer, also his man of business, bowed and backed out of the door as if leaving royalty. Everett limped across to the desk, pausing for a moment to catch his breath as the pain in his damaged leg almost overwhelmed him. Perhaps he should ensure his cane was always with him in future.

Five years ago he had been a man in his prime, with an older brother and two healthy parents and no expectations of taking on the dukedom. Then everything changed. They were returning from a ball in London when a building they were passing had collapsed, burying their vehicle beneath the debris. His family had been killed, and he horribly injured.

Since that dreadful night, he had remained in solitude at their family estate in Hertfordshire, refusing to see anyone apart from his lawyer. He had closed down most of the house and now resided in a downstairs apartment intended for an elderly relative. Stairs were things he avoided.

His only respite from his pain and misery was when he was astride his magnificent black stallion, Othello. When in the saddle, he could forget he was a cripple, and gallop about his domain as any other gentleman might do.

He spent the next few hours dealing with estate matters. None of the tenants, staff or neighbours could complain he was neglecting his duties. Despite preferring to remain a recluse he still had pride in his name and had no intention of letting his heritage fall into disarray.

One might have thought that marrying would also be part of his plans — but he had discovered there was a perfectly acceptable alternative to a child of his own. The person concerned, one Richard Hemingford, had no notion he was his heir, and Everett intended his third cousin remain in ignorance.

If this gentleman discovered what was in store for him he might wish to visit and that could not be allowed. Also, Hemingford might start dining out on his prospects, and this too would be unacceptable. Twenty years hence would be time enough to invite the future Duke of Hemingford to inspect his demesne.

★   ★   ★

Miss Lydia Sinclair gathered the four children together to explain what was to happen to all of them now their parents were gone. Her sister Sarah and her husband Jonathan had preferred to spend their time travelling to exotic places rather than remain at home taking care of their children. Hence the fact that their demise, although unfortunate, would make little difference to her nieces and nephews.

'So you see, children, we can no longer remain here, as the house belongs to the bank . . . '

'Where are we going to go? Don't we have any relatives who could take us in?' Emma always got straight to the point. She was ten years of age, but sounded and looked a lot older.

'I have been going through the papers in your papa's study, and have discovered that you are related to a duke. Your mama was his cousin, which makes you his second cousins. I have written to him telling him of our sad loss, and informing him he is now guardian to you four.'

Richard, at eight, was already holding strong opinions on most subjects, and aristocrats in particular. 'I don't want to have him take charge of us. You are our aunt; can't you be our guardian?'

'I cannot be legally in charge of your welfare, my love; it has to be the nearest male relative, and unfortunately that is the duke.' There was an uncle, but he was the black sheep of the Castleford family and had not been heard of for years. She gestured around the dilapidated chamber. 'Surely none of you would wish to remain here in such unpleasant surroundings?'

The twins had little interest in the subject — she had been their only carer, and if she was with them, they would be content. Their fourth name day was next month, and she sincerely hoped they would be settled somewhere before then.

'Anywhere will be better than this place, Aunt Lydia,' Emma said. 'Do you think we shall have to wait long for an answer to your letter?'

'I spent an exorbitant amount of money sending it express, so one would hope we would get a response by return.'

'Emma and I are going to the village — do you want anything from the shop?'

'I shall give you a penny each to spend if you take the little ones with you. I have things I want to complete this morning and cannot do so if they are with me.'

David and Lottie scrambled to their feet in happy expectation of the walk. 'Please, please, we come with you. We like walks.' As always, they spoke in unison, referring to themselves in the plural.

Lydia handed over three coppers and the children departed, eager to spend their largesse. She had put them from her mind before they had left the house. They were independent and resilient, and she was confident the older two could take care of their siblings without her interference.

If there was still a nursemaid employed she would have sent the girl with them, but the only staff remaining in the house were a cook-housekeeper, her simple daughter who acted as maid of all work, and her husband who was the outside man.

She opened the small money box in which the remainder of their income was stored. All the family had in the world to sustain them was two pounds, three shillings and sixpence. One pound of this would be given to the family, which left her the remainder to pay for their travelling costs and any other incidentals.

Her intention was to depart regardless of the response she received from the duke. He could hardly turn them away when they arrived destitute on his doorstep. She didn't like to lie to the children, but had no option. The letter had not gone by express, so wouldn't arrive for several days; therefore, they must already be on their way before any response could be sent.

Whilst the children were away, she would pack their meagre belongings into small bags they could manage between them. The next task would be to harness the ancient nag to the gig and drive herself to the coaching inn on the toll road two miles away. It would be an unpleasant and arduous journey travelling by the common stage, but she had no option. She prayed there was sufficient money to purchase inside tickets as travelling on top of the coach would be impossible.

William had anticipated her wishes and the vehicle was waiting outside. 'Want me to come with you, miss?'

'No thank you, you have more than enough to do here in my absence. I'm hoping the bank won't come to claim the house for another few days, which should give you and Ivy time to transfer everything you want to your new cottage. I wish I could do more for you, but . . . '

'Don't you worry, miss, we'll have the chickens, and enough food to keep us going. I'll be able to plant up my new garden with the seeds and sets saved from last year. And having the gig and old Freddie here as well will mean I can earn a bob or two as a carter.'

Satisfied she wouldn't be leaving William and his wife in dire financial straits, Lydia climbed onto the gig and picked up the reins. The drive to the inn was accomplished without incident and she was delighted to be able to reserve four seats on the eight o'clock coach the next day. One of the twins would be obliged to sit on her lap, but she didn't anticipate that this would be a problem.

When they returned from the village everything was ready for their departure the next day. She had decided not to inform the children until they left. In the excitement of going on their first long journey, she hoped the older two would not question her decision. Emma, if she realised they were travelling unannounced to their destination, would refuse to go. She was a girl who liked to do everything correctly — heaven knew where she got that from.

* * *

Everett had been told by his physician that there was a procedure that could be carried out on his leg to straighten it. This would allow him to walk normally and without the pain he suffered now. Doctor Adams had been serving in the army but had returned recently in order to take over his uncle's local practice.

Deciding to have this done, however painful it might be, had been an easy choice. Anything was worthwhile if it would give him back his mobility. Adams was coming this morning to discuss what would be involved.

The doctor was ushered in by the butler, Frobisher, and Everett waved him to the seat. 'Welcome, sir. I am eager to hear what you intend to do to me, and how long must I spend recuperating.'

'Essentially, I am going to break your leg again and then reset it properly. At the moment the bones are not aligned, and that's what's causing you so much pain.'

'Good God! I'd no idea you intended to do something so drastic. Does this mean I shall be confined to bed for weeks?'

'You have had so much trouble with your leg since the accident five years ago because you didn't remain stationary for long enough. You must remain in bed for three weeks, then you can use crutches as long as you keep the weight off your limb for a further three weeks.'

'Can you guarantee I will be able to walk without pain once everything has healed?'

The doctor nodded. 'That is the plan, your grace. When do you want to proceed?'

'As soon as possible; I have sufficient staff to take care of me, and I believe there is a bath chair somewhere on the premises that will be ideal.'

'I don't recommend that you use this contraption for the first three weeks, your grace. In fact, I forbid you to do so.'

Everett clenched his teeth. He wasn't accustomed to being told what to do, but if he wished this excellent surgeon to fix his leg he had no choice but to obey. 'I shall be guided by you, sir, and follow your strictures to the letter. When will you do it?'

'I wish you to spend the next few days . . . '

'No. I'm not prepared to wait any longer. Do it tomorrow, or don't do it at all and I will find someone else in your place.' Had he overplayed his hand? The young man nodded.

'Very well, your grace, I shall do as you bid. However, your recovery would be far easier if you were prepared to follow the regime I was going to suggest for a week before the operation.'

'I'll take my chances. Explain to my valet what will be needed.' He nodded his dismissal and the doctor inclined his head in turn. Everett was aware he was too brusque when dealing with his inferiors, but that was only to be expected when one was a duke. He had been brought up to expect instant obedience to his commands, and did not take kindly to anyone who ignored his requests. If he was to be confined to his apartment for the next few weeks he must be certain that his estate manager, his man of affairs, and his secretary would be able to deal with anything that arose during his incapacity.

The doctor had warned him the procedure would be excruciatingly painful, but an hour or two of agony would be worth it if he could then spend the remainder of his days with two good legs. He had all but forgotten the days when he had gone about Town with his cronies, enjoying the favours of his mistress, and indulging in the customary pastimes of wealthy and well-bred gentlemen.

If Adams worked this miracle, then perhaps he would start socialising once more. He would have the summer to recuperate, and then might open his house in Grosvenor Square, venture to London and visit his clubs so he could catch up on the world he had abandoned.

First, though, he had to get through

the next few weeks; he hoped he had the courage to do so without complaint.

★ ★ ★

'We don't want to get in, it's smelly and dirty.' David stamped his foot.

'Do as you're told, young man, or you will be left here on your own.' Lydia was hot and flustered, and not enjoying the smirks and sniggers of the other passengers as she tried to persuade the recalcitrant twins to clamber inside the coach.

Lottie had sat down on the cobbles and closed her eyes, as if by so doing she had become invisible. 'Emma, you and Richard must pick your sister up and carry her in, and I will do the same with David. We cannot keep everyone waiting a moment longer.'

This manoeuvre worked splendidly, but resulted in the most hideous cacophony of wails and screams when the little ones had had their plans thwarted. A stout matron, with a bonnet that looked more like a coal scuttle than a hat, said loudly:

'What they need is a good hiding; and if you don't do it, then someone else will.'

Lydia was drawing breath to tell this interfering old woman exactly what she thought of her suggestion when the twins stopped wriggling and screaming. There was a collective sigh of relief from the other three passengers.

'There, that always does the trick. Now we can travel in comfort.' The matron smiled, closed her eyes, and promptly fell asleep.

The little ones had stopped gulping and snuffling, and soon were also quiet. Lydia turned to her older niece and nephew. 'They are always crotchety when they have not had enough rest. Are you going to be comfortable with Lottie sprawled across you?'

They nodded and managed weak smiles, but she could see tears in their eyes. They might appear to be wise beyond their years, but they were only recently orphaned, and had been torn from everything they knew to travel to an unknown destination and an uncertain reception.

Perhaps she relied too much on their willingness to help. In the future, she wouldn't ask so much of them, but take on all responsibility for their little family herself.

★   ★   ★

The journey was accomplished without any further disruption from the twins. All the children were subdued and she understood how they felt. They had disembarked from the coach an hour ago, and she had not sufficient funds to pay for them to break their fast. They were all hungry, dirty and grumpy.

'I'm sure someone will come and collect us soon, my loves, but until then we must be patient . . . '

'We're hungry and want to relieve ourselves,' David announced loudly enough for the two gentlemen, blowing

17

a cloud outside the inn's front door, to hear. They were not amused by the comment.

'Hush, sweetheart, that's not something anyone else should hear about,' Lydia said, but she sympathised as she too had a need for the commode. They could hardly use the facilities as they were not paying customers.

The inn was surrounded by buildings, and the thoroughfare was busy with diligences, carriages and carts. There were no convenient fields or hedges they could hide behind.

Then an ostler took pity on them. 'There's a privy out the back, miss, none too clean but I don't reckon you have a choice.'

Remembering how the twins had reacted to the less-than-pleasant smell of the interior of the coach, Lydia was about to refuse. Then Lottie tugged her skirt.

'I need to go, I need to go right now.'

The fact that the little girl referred to herself only and not her brother too indicated how desperate she was. 'Thank you, we should be most grateful to use your primitive facilities.'

The experience was as unpleasant as she'd anticipated — she hoped never to have to endure such a thing again — but they were all now comfortable and able to wait without fidgeting. She had offered the kind ostler a coin, but to her embarrassment he had refused.

'You hang onto that, miss, buy the littl'uns a bun. There's a bakery a couple of doors down. They often have stale buns going cheap.'

'I shall not forget your kindness, sir, and will repay it one day when our circumstances have improved.'

Emma and Richard, with three pennies clutched in their hands, were happy to go in search of the buns whilst she did her best to distract the twins by playing word games with them. The note she had sent to Hemingford Court should have been read and understood long ago. Why didn't someone come to collect them?

'Look what we have, we've got lots and lots of good things. They were ever so kind and filled up an old basket for us.' Emma held it out triumphantly.

'Good heavens! That's a feast indeed. Shall we take it over to that corner, near the stables? Then we can sit on the boxes.'

The ostler showed Richard where there was a pump, and in turn they went and quenched their thirst. There were meat pasties, buns and cakes as well as a whole loaf she was certain wasn't yesterday's bake.

'We must not eat all of this, my dears; we must keep some for later, in case . . . in case we have to wait longer than we expect to.'

2

A further hour passed before Lydia and the children were approached by a middle-aged gentleman dressed entirely in black.

'Miss Sinclair, I must apologise for keeping you waiting, but arrangements had to be made. We did not expect you to arrive so soon. I am his grace's lawyer and man of affairs, Mr Digby, here to serve you.' He stared at the meagre pile of luggage. 'Where are your trunks? Surely this is not all the baggage you have brought with you?'

'It is, sir, as we were obliged to travel on the common stage and could not bring anything else. I am sure that the children's guardian will supply what they need.'

'He will indeed. He has set up a substantial fund for your exclusive use. You will find everything you need to know waiting for you in the library of your new home. Come along, I'm sure you are eager to see your new abode.' He led the way out of the yard to a smart carriage outside. No emblem was on the side to indicate it came from the duke — in fact, neither the coachman, nor the man by the steps, were dressed in a recognisable livery.

The children needed no urging to scramble into the vehicle. Despite their wild behaviour, there was ample room inside for the bags and themselves. Strangely, the lawyer did not accompany them; perhaps he did not like the company of children and preferred to travel on his own.

'Are we going to live in a palace or a castle?' Lottie asked.

'I've no idea, sweetheart, but I'm sure a duke's house will be substantial even if it isn't a palace or a castle.'

The children rushed from one side to the other of the carriage, making it rock alarmingly but she was too dispirited and weary to correct them. She closed her eyes and tried to gather her thoughts. Her parents had perished from the sweating sickness when she was young, so she had spent her formative years in the household of her older sister Sarah. Lydia had been largely ignored, and no provision had been made for her formal education: what she knew, she had gleaned for herself in the library.

As soon as she was old enough to take responsibility for her nieces and nephews, her sister and brother-in-law had more or less abandoned their children and left the upbringing of them to her. She had taught the older ones to read and write, to figure, to draw, and to use the globe. For the past year she had allowed Emma and Richard to wander about the neighbourhood on their own. Taking care of the twins was more than enough for her.

Then the news had come through that Sarah and her husband had drowned somewhere in the Indian

Ocean, leaving nothing. Lydia had eventually discovered the will and saw that the Duke of Hemingford was now responsible for his second cousins. She prayed he would be happy to assume responsibility for her as well, otherwise she was destitute.

Now, here they were, being driven in a smart carriage to Hemingford Court. They looked little better than ragamuffins, and she hoped they would not be turned away as unsuitable for such a prestigious place.

She was dragged from her reverie by the twins beginning to fight in the well of the carriage. In the melee of flailing arms and legs she had been soundly kicked on the ankle. 'Stop that, you two, this minute!' She reached down, dragged them apart, and positioned one on either side of her so they couldn't continue the struggle.

'Emma, Richard, I'm disappointed in both of you. You should have stopped this altercation before it started.'

Emma had been staring morosely out

of the window; whilst her brother, looking equally miserable, was sitting opposite doing the same thing. Something was not right.

Lydia finally took notice of their passage and was shocked to see they were approaching a substantial, but neglected, building that certainly wasn't the home of any duke.

Before she could comment the vehicle rocked to a standstill and the door was opened by a waiting servant. There was no sign of Mr Digby. It couldn't have been made more plain — they were not wanted and were being hidden away in a property that obviously hadn't been occupied for some time.

She straightened her shoulders and pinned on a bright smile. 'I can't tell you how relieved I am, children, not to be obliged to stay at the main house. We shall do much better here on our own. When we do meet your guardian, we shall be well-dressed and will make a better impression.'

The older children perked up and exchanged glances. 'We didn't think of that, Aunt Lydia. We do look like poor relations at the moment.'

Richard giggled. 'That's what we are, silly; but in a week or two, everything will be different.'

'We are better off already, aren't we? We had no servants to look after us before,' Emma said.

'Exactly so, my dear. Shall we go in and see our new home?'

As they reached the dirty front steps, the door opened and two less than-friendly-figures emerged. The woman was tall and thin, and smartly dressed in dark blue bombazine; the man shorter and wider, but equally smart.

Lydia's cheeks coloured as they stared at her superciliously. If one was to judge on appearances, it was she and not they who was the servant. She would not be intimidated. She was the granddaughter of a lord; not as well-connected to the nobility as her nieces and nephews, who were related to a duke, but still not of the lower classes.

'I am Miss Sinclair. I am mistress here. You will arrange for a substantial meal to be set out in the dining room in one hour. Before that, we wish to be shown our accommodation and have hot water sent up.' She waited for them to acknowledge this order before continuing. 'You will assemble any staff employed at this establishment in the hall at six o'clock. Is that quite clear?'

The man, presumably the butler, inclined his head an inch, but the woman remained impassive.

The four children were hiding behind her, uncertain of their new environment. Lydia had no intention of saying exactly what she felt with the youngsters present — they had had more than enough upset in their lives recently. However, these two would get their comeuppance, that was for sure.

A nervous maid conducted them to the first floor, but instead of stopping there she continued towards the narrow, uncarpeted staircase that led to a less salubrious part of the house.

'Children, shall we find ourselves suitable chambers?' Lydia ignored the maid, who was hopping from foot to foot at the bottom of the stairs, expecting her to follow.

None of the rooms were ready for occupancy, but after they had rushed about removing the holland covers they were all thrilled with what they saw.

'This one has a dressing room and a sitting room, Aunt Lydia; you must reside here,' Emma said.

'I shall indeed; it is far grander than I am accustomed to, but I'm sure I will soon adjust to my elevated status.'

Emma decided she would share with the twins, and selected another bed-chamber adjacent to the one that Lydia had chosen. In this there were two large beds: ideal for the three of them.

'I'm going in here, Aunt Lydia,' Richard said gleefully, 'it's on the other side of you and has a communicating door. Why is this there?'

'This must be the master suite, my love; the lady of the house would take the room you're having, and the gentleman the one that I've got. The first thing we must do is strip the beds as the sheets will be damp.' Then she reconsidered her statement. 'Can you see a bell-strap anywhere, children? The first person to find one has my permission to pull it as hard as they like.'

Richard found it first, and yanked it so hard he was smothered by a cloud of plaster from the ceiling. They were all laughing when two maids appeared from the dressing room. There was obviously a servants' entrance in there somewhere.

'I wish to know your names.'

The oldest girl, with mousy brown hair, curtsied. 'I am Sally, madam, and this is Jen.'

'Good. I wish to have these rooms prepared for us. The beds need to be aired and remade, and everywhere must be dusted and the floors swept. We shall return in an hour and expect it to be done.'

They both curtsied again, and she gathered the children and left the servants to do their job. 'We shall explore our new home whilst we wait for our meal to be served. Mr Digby told me there are documents and so on in the library, and I wish to know what is in them.'

The children bounced around the corridor, exclaiming and laughing at the things they saw. The house had obviously been unoccupied for several years, but with a little attention it would be a delightful place in which to live. If she was honest, she would far prefer to live in obscurity in this house than in full view of the children's illustrious relative in the other.

What she discovered in the library was far better than she could ever have hoped for. There was a large bag of golden guineas for her incidental expenses — more money than she had seen in her lifetime. There was also a letter giving her *carte blanche* to employ or dismiss any of the staff, and to add further servants if she so wished. Bills for household expenses, clothes, etcetera were to be handed on to him at the end of each quarter for payment.

The children had settled down quite happily with a selection of books taken from the library shelves. There was certainly more than enough here to keep them occupied for several years. A polite tap on the door heralded the arrival of the maid she had first encountered, the one who had tried to take them to the nursery floor.

'If you would care to come with me, miss, there is a cold collation served in the breakfast parlour.'

'What is your name? I like to know the identity of those who serve me.'

The girl dipped. 'I'm Mary, miss, at your service.'

Emma scrabbled to her feet and came over. 'What are the names of the housekeeper and butler?'

'Mrs Evans and Mr Rushton, miss.'

Lydia was pleased her niece had asked this question, as it wasn't an enquiry she could make herself. As the mistress of this house, it was imperative that she appeared to be in charge — not knowing the names of senior servants would put her at a disadvantage. That this was deliberate on their part, she was certain.

The repast set out for them was everything it should be, and they all enjoyed it. Eventually everyone was replete, chins were wiped, and the twins looked ready for bed.

'Our rooms will be ready for us now, my loves, shall we go up? I think David and Lottie can retire now; but Emma, you and Richard can stay up for another hour or two. However, I need you to stay upstairs whilst I speak to Evans and Rushton.'

There was no need for her to explain further; they were bright children, and knew she intended to dismiss both these unpleasant characters. That she would then have to run the house herself until she could find replacements did not bother her one jot — she was well-used to being in charge of a household, but had never had such generous funds at her disposal.

⋆ ⋆ ⋆

Everett was slowly recovering from the operation to reset his leg. The first few days had been as bad as anything he'd endured before, but now, a week later, he was in less pain than he had been for years.

He had become resigned to being bedridden for another two weeks, and was spending the time reading books from his long-neglected library. As far as he knew, his estate and household were running smoothly, and Digby was dealing with all the day-to-day matters as they might arise.

The doctor was delighted with his progress, and had said he could be transferred to the bath chair and wheeled outside to the terrace in another week. This was a week earlier than expected, and for the first time since the accident Everett was feeling more optimistic about his future. The use of crutches would be forbidden for another two weeks, but just being allowed outside in the early summer sunshine was enough to raise his spirits.

Fortunately, he had become accustomed to his own company, and was quite content without visitors. His doctor diligently appeared each morning to check the leg was healing, and on the third visit Everett invited him to remain and share a jug of coffee and pastries with him.

So their friendship developed — an unlikely alliance between two disparate gentlemen. Adams was, it transpired, the same age as him, but there the similarities ended. Everett had grown up the petted younger son of one of the warmest men in England, whereas Adams was the eldest son of a vicar. His education and training had been a struggle financially for his family.

'They must be proud, sir, to see you working so successfully in your chosen profession.'

'They are, your grace, and I am slowly repaying them the money they were obliged to spend on my behalf.' He smiled. 'Of course, I have been able to pay back a substantial sum this month.'

'If I had any contact with my neighbours, I should recommend your services to them.' Everett returned the smile in full measure. 'Feel free to bandy about your connection with such an illustrious gentleman as myself if by so doing it improves your income.'

When Adams departed an hour later, Everett was well satisfied with the visit. Tomorrow he was being allowed to use the bath chair. His valet, Michaels, had refurbished this ancient contraption, and it now worked as good as new.

The following morning his man assisted him into a specially prepared set of breeches — they had had the left leg cut to accommodate the splints and bandages. Over these he wore a lawn shirt and a loosely-tied neckcloth. He was immaculately shaven, and his hair had been neatly brushed and gathered at the back of his neck with a ribbon. This old-fashioned style suited him, and he had no intention of aping fashionable styles by having it cut short.

'Are you ready, your grace?' Michaels asked him.

'I am. Should we not wait for Adams to arrive?'

'He said that you could go outside today, but didn't specify the hour. If you would care to put your arm around my neck, your grace, I'll assist you into the chair.'

A young footman had been designated to hold his damaged leg so that it didn't suffer from the transfer. The manoeuvre was completed smoothly and he felt no pain at all.

'I shall break my fast outside. Is the table that I asked for set up out there?'

'Everything is as you requested, your grace.'

Michaels snapped his fingers and the young footman grabbed hold of the handles at the back of the bath chair. To his astonishment, Everett found himself travelling at high speed across the polished boards, and for a terrifying moment expected to be catapulted from his precarious position inside the vehicle.

His valet raced ahead and threw his weight onto the front of the bath chair — together the two of them managed to prevent an accident. Everett released his grip on the sides of the basketwork. 'God's teeth! You nearly had me out then — what the devil were you thinking?'

'I beg your pardon, your grace; I expected it to be hard to shift, but it flew away with me.'

'Make damn sure it doesn't happen again.'

He was wheeled with more circumspection to the table which had been laid up for breakfast at the far side of the terrace. Only as he approached did he realise he would be unable to reach the plate and cutlery because the bath chair was much lower than a normal chair. He waited to see what his two attendants would do about this conundrum.

'I'll fetch you a side table, your grace,' Michaels said, and promptly rushed off to get it.

'Put my chair in the shade — it's going to be hot later on.'

Within one quarter of an hour, everything was arranged to his satisfaction. The coffee jug was within arm's reach on the side table, and the young footman, Bates, remained close by but out of sight, ready to answer his every demand.

When Dr Adams arrived at his usual time he showed no surprise to find his patient already ensconced on the terrace.

'I'm pleased to see you here, your grace, and looking more alert and a better colour than you have for the past two weeks.' He didn't wait to be invited to help himself to pastries and coffee or to take a seat; they were on familiar terms now.

'I intend to stay out here all day; in fact, I shall be here until I am able to walk about unaided. I shall, of course, use my crutches when you say I am allowed, but until then I'm content to sit here.'

'Your progress has been nothing short of remarkable, your grace. I wish all my patients made so speedy a recovery.'

They chatted about the price of corn, the problem with unemployed return- ing soldiers, and other matters of interest until the doctor took his leave.

'I shall not continue to visit daily, your grace, there's no need. I shall come again in two days' time and hopefully get you onto your feet.'

3

Lydia was pleased with her progress at the Dower House. She had dismissed the unpleasant butler and his cohort, and promoted the single footman to his old position. It turned out that the cook had a friend expert in household matters who she appointed as the new housekeeper.

She now had her own personal maid — again, on recommendation from Cook. A further two girls from the village joined the staff, and Sally and Jen became nursemaids to the twins. The house had been scrubbed, polished and dusted from top to bottom, vases had been filled with flowers, and the kitchen garden had been taken in hand.

All they needed now were some chickens, two yard cats, and perhaps a house cow to supply fresh milk, butter and cheese. Emma and Richard were like different children — outgoing, always smiling and rarely in the house. She knew she should insist they did some schoolwork every day but had not the heart to curtail their enjoyment. She would curb their leisure time in a few weeks but for now they could roam free.

The little ones were equally content. Having two cheerful nursemaids at their beck and call was something they revelled in. They too were out of doors more than they were in. This gave her the time she needed to get on with writing her novel. It had always been her dearest wish to become a published author. Now that she had the where-withal to pay for publication, if she could not find a company who would take her on and pay her for the privilege, then she was determined to complete the book and take it to London herself.

She was engrossed in her writing in the library when she was interrupted by the arrival of Mr Digby.

'My dear Miss Sinclair, I am delighted to see you looking so well. You have worked miracles in this house in the short time you have been living here.' He glanced at the papers scattered on the desk and her ink-stained fingers. 'I beg your pardon, my dear, have I come at an inopportune moment?'

'No, sir, I am delighted to see you. There is something most particular I wish to ask you.' She stood up and joined him on the other side of the desk. 'My dearest wish is to have my novel published. I shall have completed it in a few weeks, but have no notion to whom I should send it when it's done.'

He was looking somewhat sceptical. 'I assume it is of a romantic nature, Miss Sinclair?'

'Indeed it is — but also full of adventure as well. I am cognisant of the fact that I am unlikely to find a publisher willing to take me on. However, as I shall not be spending any money on replacing my wardrobe, I intend to use that to pay, if necessary, for the publication myself.'

He pursed his lips. 'I think you might do better, my dear, concentrating on your appearance instead of wasting your money on such an enterprise.'

'I care not how I look, sir; I have no intention of marrying. A young lady only dresses to impress a gentleman, does she not? So you must see that there is no necessity for me to bother about my appearance. My clothes are clean and serviceable, and that is quite enough for me.'

He looked unconvinced. 'I'm not sure that his grace would approve of you spending his money in such a way, my dear. It is provided for the benefit of the children, not for such a frivolous venture.'

'His grace has made it very plain that he wishes to have nothing to do with any of us. I'm quite happy to act as mother to the children until they are old enough to take care of themselves. I am suitably grateful that the duke is prepared to provide for me until I'm no longer needed. Therefore, you must understand that before that time comes, I should be self-sufficient.'

His bushy black eyebrows shot up under his hair. 'Good heavens, Miss Sinclair, you must not think his grace will cast you out when your duties are done. You will be well provided for, so there's no need to pursue this further.' He warmed to his theme. 'I must also reassure you about the other matter, that of the children's welfare. At the moment his grace has serious health problems, but when he's recovered, I can assure you he will be taking a keen interest in his wards.'

Somewhat disconcerted by his vehemence, Lydia did not respond immediately. The last thing she wanted was for the duke to take any sort of interest in any of them — and especially not a keen one.

'I apologise if I sounded ungrateful, Mr Digby. His grace has done everything he ought, apart from take us into his own home. I had no notion he was a sickly gentleman. I can understand now why he didn't wish for us to reside with him. Four lively children would not be beneficial to a gentleman suffering from ill health.'

'Exactly so: you have grasped the situation perfectly, my dear. If you are content to remain here, then I am sure that his grace will be content to leave matters as they are.' He smiled benevolently and nodded towards the scattered papers. 'As to this other business, I shall say no more about it. If you do not overspend your allowance, then I am sure his grace can have no objection to your using it on whatever project you wish.'

'Thank you, sir, I give you my word there will be nothing untoward in my accounts. I do beg your pardon, I have been remiss in my duties as hostess. Can I offer you any refreshments?'

'I thank you, but I have to be elsewhere. If you would care to hand me any bills you might have received over these past two weeks, I shall be on my way.'

Once this transaction was completed he departed, promising to return in four weeks. She was to contact him at his office at Hemingford Court if she encountered any problems.

★   ★   ★

Everett was dozing in the shade on the terrace when he heard the unmistakable sound of children's voices coming from somewhere in the trees that run along the edge of the park. He pushed himself upright and squinted into the sunshine, but at first he couldn't see them. Then two small shapes became distinguishable in the shrubbery at the edge of the park on that side of the house.

He had lived here all his life, and as far as he was aware, no village child had ever had the temerity to venture onto his land without permission. He didn't like children — in fact he preferred animals to humans, even adult ones.

His three wolfhounds were sprawled at his feet, always ready to do his bidding. 'Benji, go seek.' He gestured towards the woods and the largest of the three raced away, long pink tongue lolling from the side of his open mouth.

No sooner had he given his command than he regretted his actions. The animal wouldn't harm the intruders, but he might well cause them to be terrified — for there were not many adults, let alone children, who were not intimidated by the size of his dogs.

He cursed, and the young footman appeared by magic at his side. 'Something wrong, your grace?'

'There are village urchins in the trees over there, and I sent Benji to investigate. Go after him and bring him back before he causes them undue distress.'

He could have yelled at his dog to return, but that would have been undignified. A duke must always remember his position in the world.

The young man set off willingly after

the dog. Everett shaded his eyes from the sun, but couldn't see the children or his animal. If any harm had come to them because of his actions, he would never forgive himself. He must pray that they had just run off and his hound had followed.

After an anxious wait, the red-faced footman returned. 'I couldn't find the hound or the children, your grace. Shall I send someone from the stables to look for them?'

'Take me inside first, then do that. What is your name? If you are to wheel me about for the next week or so, I need to know this.'

'Bates, your grace.' The young man bowed.

'Have you been employed here long?'

'Two years this September, your grace.'

Michaels helped Everett onto the daybed, and Bates hurried off to the stables. If this footman had been working here so long how was it that he didn't know his name — in fact, didn't even recognise him? This would not do; there were only a dozen or so employed here: he should know all their names and faces.

In future, he would do better. Indeed, once he was on his feet he would replenish his wardrobe, revamp the main wing of the house, and get Frobisher to engage a full complement of staff. When this was done, he might even consider inviting his neighbours to dinner. That was if they cared to renew their acquaintance — it was five years since he had interacted with any of his peers.

Bates came back to tell him two outside men had gone in search of the missing dog. Benji was the most independent of the three, and frequently wandered off, so Everett was not unduly bothered by his continued absence.

The three hounds he kept as his companions were all male — the breeding bitches were housed outside. There was a constant demand for the puppies, and his kennelman made sure every litter was the best it could be. There was also a small stud on the estate — he had two magnificent stallions and half a dozen broodmares. The progeny from these were also sold for a tidy sum at Tattersalls in London. He had no need of the extra money, but enjoyed the challenge of breeding a horse that would impress its owner.

*   *   *

'We should not go in the woods, Richard, it will be trespassing,' Emma said.

'No it's not — we have as much right to be in there as anyone else. The duke's our guardian, isn't he?'

'He is, but he doesn't want to know us, and I'm sure he would be most displeased if he found us in his woods. And Aunt Lydia will be even more cross if she was ever to find out we had strayed so far.'

Her brother ignored her concerns

and continued along the narrow path so she had no option but to follow him.

They climbed a few trees and scared a few pheasants, before realising they were lost. 'We promised to be back for luncheon, Richard, and it must be well past midday now. I told you we should never have come in here.'

Her brother pointed to the sunlight filtering in through the trees a little way ahead. 'We will be out of the trees soon, and then can find our way home easily.'

She did not have his confidence, but ran after him, calling for him to slow down as she wasn't sure they were going to emerge on the correct side of the wood.

He stopped, turned around, and yelled at her: 'We've been going in the wrong direction, Emma; we are on the edge of the park, and I can see the duke's house.'

She waved, hoping he would understand her gesture and stop shouting. Voices carried across an empty space in a way they didn't when in the middle of a forest.

On arriving at his side, she stood in wonder and gazed at the magnificent building. 'I believe there must be hundreds of windows. I think it would take an hour to walk from one end to the other.'

He moved closer to her, needing her reassurance in the face of such splendour. 'I think I would get lost if I was living there, Emma. I much prefer it where we are. I'm glad he didn't want us.'

The grounds appeared to be deserted, as was the terrace that ran along the length of this wing of the edifice. There was a wall encasing the terrace at the end nearest to them, and she shuddered at the thought there might be someone lurking behind it.

'Look at those steps, and see, there's a maze over there — at least, I think that's what it is. Shall we go and investigate?'

'No, we must go home at once before

we're discovered.' She took his arm and pulled him back to the trees. He grumbled as they tried to retrace their steps and find the narrow path that would lead them back into the gardens of the Dower House.

She froze. A large animal was chasing them and it was too late to run.

Was there time to climb a tree? Were there wild boar in this wood? She dragged her brother behind a tree and pushed him into the branches. Not a moment too soon, as a huge brindled hound bounded into view. The dog was wagging its tail and stood upright on its hind legs in an effort to reach them.

'It doesn't look fierce, Emma, it looks really friendly.' Before she could prevent him, her brother slithered down the trunk and threw his arms around the huge beast's neck.

'Good boy, good boy, have you come to show us the way home?'

Emma joined him on the ground; the dog licked her hand and nudged her with his massive head. 'You are a lovely fellow! Stop licking me and let me have a good look at you. Sit, boy.'

The dog obeyed her instruction immediately. 'He must have heard us calling and has come to help,' Richard insisted.

She wasn't so sure; she feared that close behind this animal would be his owner. They would be discovered and severely punished for their misbehaviour.

'Go home, boy, go home at once.'

This instruction, the dog ignored. He remained sitting on the dirt — even in this position he was almost as tall as her brother.

'We want to go home to the Dower House, boy, can you show us the way?'

'He won't know what you're saying, Richard, and I think we'd better get away from here before we are found.'

The animal licked her hand again, and then was on its feet and sniffing the ground. Then he trotted forward, glancing over his shoulder as if to see they were following him.

'See, I told you he was clever and could take us home.'

As she had no idea in which direction to go, she thought they might as well follow the dog after all, for they could not be more lost than they already were.

Fifteen minutes later, they were back where they had started earlier that day. Richard flung his arms around the dog and kissed him. Emma did the same. They fussed him for a while, and then reluctantly told him to go home.

'Quickly, I can hear Sally shouting for us. We have been away too long.' She grabbed her brother's hand, pulling him through the shrubbery and across the grass to the back door. 'Don't say anything about the dog; we must just say we forgot the time.'

He looked over his shoulder. 'He's gone; he will find his way home without any trouble. He follows his nose, you know.'

Aunt Lydia was not impressed by their late appearance. 'You will go to your room immediately and remain there the rest of the day. I am most displeased with you both. If you can't be trusted to remain in the grounds and return when you hear the clock strike twelve for your luncheon, then you must remain where you can be seen.'

'I'm sorry, Aunt Lydia, we promise we won't do it again. It's such fun here, it's easy to forget we should come home.'

Her brother echoed her apology. 'I'm sorry too; we didn't intend to worry you or cause you any trouble.'

'Very well, I shall say no more about it this time. You will go upstairs, wash the dirt from your person, and then spend the remainder of the day writing an account of what you did. You may draw a picture to go with it if you wish.'

Once they were safely upstairs, Emma breathed a sigh of relief. 'We were lucky this time, Richard, but we must be more circumspect in future.'

Being obliged to remain indoors on such a lovely day was a severe punishment, but Emma thought they deserved it. They were given permission to play with the twins before the little ones went to their beds.

Sally had doused the last candle and Emma was completing her prayers when her brother crept in. 'You must come with me — I can hear the dog crying in the garden. I think he might be hurt.'

★   ★   ★

When Everett retired, the missing dog had still not returned. He told Bates that if the animal was not safely home by morning, then the search must be widened. It was, of course, possible a poacher had taken him. Benji was a gentle giant, fierce if he needed to be, but if approached softly he would respond in kind.

He was also valuable, and anyone prepared to risk the gallows or transportation by poaching on the duke's land would not think twice about stealing the dog. When he discovered the culprit, they would regret their rash action.

For the first time in years, he slept well, and woke the next morning eager to face the day. He was less sanguine when he discovered his favourite hound was still missing.

'I want every available man out searching. Make sure the gamekeeper is aware, as he too can help. Every cottage and house in the village and surrounding countryside must be investigated. I will have my dog back by the end of the day.'

4

Lydia become so engrossed in her writing that it wasn't until the candles flickered and went out she understood how late it was. She had not closed the shutters in the library, so there was sufficient moonlight filtering in for her to see perfectly well. Her staff were abed long ago, as she didn't ask them to keep the same strange hours as she did. She walked across to the window, which was open, and leaned out to listen to the sound of the nightingales singing in the trees that ran around the boundary of the grounds.

Good heavens! Whatever was that dreadful noise? The hair on the back of her neck stood to attention, and her hands clenched on the windowsill. Then she relaxed as she recognised the sound. There was a canine trapped somewhere and it was whining for attention.

A sensible young lady would have exited through the front door, but she just hopped over the windowsill and went in search of the animal. 'Where are you, old fellow? I'm coming to help you — shush now, or you will wake everybody up.'

In answer the dog began to yelp excitedly, and she followed the noise to the stables. As yet, these were unoccupied by any horses, although she had every intention of purchasing ponies for the children and a riding horse for herself. The cob which pulled the gig lived outside in the meadow.

A sudden scuttle in the shadows made her jump. It sounded as if the place was alive with rodents. What they needed were a couple of cats — she really must spend more time managing her small household and less on her novel.

The dog was scratching behind a closed door. She unlatched it, and was knocked flat as two massive front paws landed on her. The huge animal then compounded his offence by attempting to lick her face.

'Get off me, you silly beast! I must get to my feet, and cannot do so with you on top of me.'

The animal cocked his head as if listening to her, and then the weight was gone and she was free to rise. Two small shapes erupted from the darkness, and Emma and Richard flung themselves onto her lap.

'Are you hurt, Aunt Lydia? We saw him knock you over,' Emma said.

'What are you both doing down here at this time of night?'

Richard replied, 'We heard the dog crying, and came down to see if we could help.' The child hesitated as if he had something else to say, but his sister glared at him, and he said nothing else.

'Well, the dog obviously got shut in somehow. Fetch him some water, both of you, and then we shall send him on his way.'

The animal drank greedily, but then refused to depart despite their encouragement and shooing. Eventually, Lydia abandoned the attempt. 'We cannot remain out here any longer, my loves; we must return to our beds. The dog has water and is free to go whenever he wishes. He brought himself here and I'm sure he can take himself back from whence he came.'

The front door stood wide open — her niece and nephew had come out the correct way. Before she could stop him, the hound bounded ahead of them and vanished into the house, much to the delight of the children.

They ran ahead, and had the good sense not to start shouting for the animal to return. 'Quickly, off to bed, I shall look for the dog and put him outside.'

'Good night, Aunt Lydia, we shall see you in the morning.' They scampered up the stairs, leaving her alone in the entrance hall.

She returned to the library, closed

the window, and with a candlestick in one hand looked for the wretched animal. He was nowhere to be found, and she was obliged to abandon the search. It would be light soon, and she had yet to have any sleep. The twins always rushed into her bedchamber as soon as they were awake, regardless of the fact that they had their own nursemaids to take care of them nowadays.

The dog was a handsome beast, well-groomed and well-fed — presumably not the property of a villager or tenant. Therefore, she decided, he must belong to the duke's kennels. She would send him home with the gardener's boy tomorrow.

As she was falling asleep, it did occur to her that if the hound was valuable — which he obviously was — they would be looking for him. He might as well remain with them until someone came to claim him.

The next morning, she was awoken by the curtains being drawn back and the delicious aroma of hot chocolate wafting towards her. For a moment she revelled in the sensation, then her heart sank. 'Mary, what time is it? Why haven't the little ones come to see me as they always do?'

'Don't you worry, miss, the twins are with Miss Emma and Master Richard. They're playing on the grass with that big dog they found yesterday.'

Lydia scrambled out of bed and ran to the window. Sure enough, all four children were there throwing sticks, and the dog was fetching them back. Each time he returned, he sat by the person who had pitched it, and dropped it politely at their feet. It didn't matter whether it was one of the little ones or Emma or Richard. He was as polite and gentle with all of them.

She had never seen them so happy and, despite his size, she hoped no one would claim him and they could keep him for their own. It was possible he was one of several dogs kept in the kennels at Hemingford Court, and that the kennelmaster could be persuaded to let him stay. After all, being at the Dower House was almost the same as being at Hemingford Court.

* * *

The first thing that Everett asked was whether Benji had returned. The response was negative, and he sent for the man most likely to give him a sensible answer. The other two older hounds appeared unbothered by the absence of the younger dog. If he was honest, they had never really taken to this new addition to his canine circle.

Once he was dressed, he demanded to be pushed to the kennels where he could speak to the man in charge. The journey across the cobbled yard was uncomfortable, and several times he feared he would be tipped out, much to the amusement of those who happened to be in the vicinity. Word of his coming had spread ahead, and the man he wanted to speak to emerged and immediately doffed his cap.

'Well, man, have you no news for me? It's not like Benji to stay away so long.'

The kennelmaster, who was shuffling nervously from foot to foot, cleared his throat before answering. 'I've got a dozen men looking for him, your grace. They will find him soon enough and bring him back.'

'I think it possible he followed the children. I didn't get a clear look at them, but one was a girl, the other a smaller boy. They were urchins from the village, I expect; it shouldn't be hard to find them. If he is with them, then just reclaim him. There's no need for anything further to be done.'

'And if he's been taken by an adult?'

'Then you know what to do. I'll have no thievery on my land.' He twisted his head so he could speak to Bates. 'Now we are out here, do think you could push me to the stud? It's been too long since I visited.'

'I'll give it a go, your grace, but I'm not sure this old thing will hold together if we go over any more cobbles and such.'

'Then take me back to the terrace.'

The following day, the dog had still not been located, and Everett was becoming more concerned as the hours passed. The reason his men hadn't found Benji must be because the dog was no longer in the neighbourhood. The animal was valuable, and whoever had got him would be thinking himself fortunate. He'd not be so happy when he was apprehended — and he would be eventually, however long it took.

The duke was not renowned for his good humour, and today he was even more irascible — and less than delighted when the butler announced that he had visitors.

'Tell them to go to the devil, I will see no one.'

Frobisher went to deliver this message, leaving him to his black thoughts. He should be more sanguine: his leg was healing well, the weather was fine, and he was outside enjoying the fresh air. For the first time in five years he was without pain — surely that should be enough to raise his spirits?

He straightened in the bath chair. There was the sound of scuffling on the other side of the terrace wall. Before he had time to summon assistance, two children and their nursemaid arrived at his side.

The boy bowed, the girl and the nursemaid curtsied.

'I beg your pardon for disturbing you, your grace, but as your butler would not allow us to come in, we have been obliged to find another way speak to you.'

His eyes widened. This was no nursemaid, but a well-bred young lady. The children looked vaguely familiar, as if he had met them somewhere before.

'We are ever so sorry, your grace, but your dog followed us. We tried to bring him back to you, but when we got near he ran off.' The girl dipped again; her face was pale, and she was clutching the hand of the young woman.

He was on the point of apologising for his ill humour when the young lady spoke again. 'My niece and nephew have come of their own volition to return your dog, your grace. I do not see the need for you to glare at them.'

The children moved smartly behind their aunt, as well they might. Nobody spoke to him so impertinently.

Then, what had been said previously finally registered. 'Devil take it! You are the brats I've inherited. What are you doing here?'

The boy was emboldened to step out from behind his aunt. 'We told you, sir: we have come to try and return your dog.'

He shook his head. 'No, why are you in this neighbourhood?'

'We arrived a while ago, your grace, and Mr Digby settled us in the Dower House. We are very comfortable there, thank you very much.'

The girl appeared. 'We much prefer it there, your grace, and have no wish to live with you.'

They were interrupted by the arrival of Bates. 'Begging your pardon, your grace, but your dog has been seen halfway down the drive. If anyone approaches, he vanishes into the woods.'

'We told you, sir; we tried to bring him back, but he just won't come.' The girl moved away from the protection of her aunt and came to stand trustingly beside him. 'We got lost in your woods the other day, and he took us home. The twins love him, and so do we.'

'Your grace, I believe your hound has formed an attachment to the children, and unless you keep him chained up he will constantly come back to them. Would you consider allowing him to live with us? After all, he would still be on your property, would he not?'

The two youngsters were staring at him imploringly; now he understood why they looked familiar. They were the urchins he'd seen the other day. When he had told Digby to take care of the matter of his unwanted wards, he'd had no idea the man intended to put them in the Dower House — but it was too late to repine. As long as they remained there, he was satisfied with the arrangement.

'Your names, if you please.'

The girl curtsied. 'I'm Emma, I am ten years of age; and this is my brother Richard, and he is eight. The twins, Charlotte and David, are at home, and they will celebrate their fourth name day next month.'

The young woman nodded in his direction. 'I am their aunt; my name is Lydia Sinclair. My nieces and nephews have been in my charge for the past four years. I have a letter from my sister and her husband making me responsible for them in the event of their death.'

★   ★   ★

For a gentleman who apparently suffered from ill health, the duke appeared remarkably robust despite being confined to a chair with wheels. She waited politely for him to respond to the startling announcement that she had been given control over her nieces and nephews.

'As I have no wish to involve myself in their upbringing, Miss Sinclair, you have my permission to continue to act as their guardian and mentor. I am more concerned, however, about the absence of my favourite hound.'

The children exchanged glances, and then Emma left the sanctuary of her skirts and went to stand beside him. She spoke slowly and clearly as if conversing with a simpleton.

'Your grace, your dog is hiding in the woods. Your dog does not want to come back. We cannot get your dog to . . . '

'Enough of your prattling, child.'

Unfortunately, Lydia attracted his attention by her smothered snigger. He was obviously not accustomed to being laughed at. She watched him take a deep breath and force his mouth into a semblance of a smile.

'Girl, take that bell and ring it loudly in the doorway.'

Obediently, Emma did as he requested, and the summons was answered immediately by a flustered-looking footman.

'I take it you've had no success reclaiming my dog?'

'No, your grace, he's still hiding somewhere.'

'Then you must wheel me around and let me call him. I'm certain he will come to me.'

Lydia should have remained silent, but couldn't prevent the words from popping out. 'I beg your pardon, your grace, but I believe you are not quite grasping the point. The dog wishes to remain with the children. He would be at your side now, would he not, if he wished to be?'

His eyes narrowed and his mouth became a hard line. She swallowed the lump in her throat but refused to apologise. She had done nothing wrong — she was merely being helpful.

'I suggest that you remain silent, unless you have something pertinent to say.'

She was about to respond to his less-than-polite comment, but thought better of it. It would not be a sound notion to anger him further, as he held their destiny in his hands. Instead, she lowered her gaze and curtsied politely.

Both Emma and Richard were standing behind her — they too must think the duke a formidable character. She risked a quick look in his direction. It appeared he had already forgotten they were there, as his harassed attendant was wheeling him in through the double doors back into the house.

'Do you think that our dog will go back to him if he calls?' Emma asked anxiously.

'I very much hope not, my dear. I would like to see his grace put soundly in his place.'

'If I was a dog, I wouldn't want to live here. I don't like the duke, he's fierce and bad-tempered,' Richard said as he skipped ahead down the terrace steps.

'Look, Aunt Lydia, I can see our dog lying down under the shrubbery over there. I hope he doesn't rush across to join us, as someone from the duke's staff will surely catch him and take him away.'

She saw where Emma was pointing. 'Yes, I can see him. I can also hear his grace arriving in his contraption. I think we had better make ourselves scarce.'

She took them back onto the terrace so that they could, if they crouched down, peer over the top of the wall without being seen by either the dog or his true owner.

They had only just got settled when three men and the duke, plus his attendant, arrived on the drive. Although she was expecting him to shout, she was unprepared for the loudness of his voice when he did call for his animal. At least they now knew the dog was called Benji — indeed, she was quite sure that anyone within miles of this location would be equally aware of this fact.

She held her breath. The dog remained where he was, and she sighed. 'I don't think he's going to come, however much he's called. We should go home now. I don't think we will be very popular after what we have just witnessed.'

'If we go back the way we came, he will see us, Aunt Lydia,' Richard said.

'Then we must lurk here until we see him come in and then make our escape. Benji will no doubt follow us when we walk past. We have done our duty; his grace knows where his animal is. If he cares to send his men to attempt to capture him, then we shall not get in their way.' The children looked dubious. 'I said, *attempt* to capture him, my dears, I am certain they would be unsuccessful.'

After a few more shouts, each one more furious than the previous, the duke abandoned his quest to bring the dog to his side. In fact, Benji was no longer in the bushes.

Richard was keeping watch, and waved his hand frantically to indicate it was time to make a rapid departure. Lydia picked up her skirts and, with the children laughing beside her, took the steps two at a time. They raced across the grass, not stopping until they reached the safety of the trees.

She was still recovering her breath when the dog joined them. From his frantic tail-wagging, it was quite clear he approved of their arrival. Richard and Emma threw their arms around his neck.

'Good, Benji, good boy. You shall come home with us and have a big bone from the kitchen for being so clever.' She had never seen her nephew look so happy, and was determined, whatever it took, that Benji would remain at the Dower House.

5

Everett was fuming. 'Take as many men as necessary and bring that dog back here. Not today, go first thing tomorrow when the house is asleep. He will be locked in an outbuilding somewhere, and easy to capture.'

The kennelman touched his cap and nodded. 'We can get him right enough, your grace, but as soon as we let him out he will be back there again. I have seen it happen before. Once a hound has made up his mind, there's no changing it.'

He waved the man away. What he said made sense — it was exactly the same thing as that wretched girl had said earlier. The sensible thing would be to agree that his dog could live with the children, but he wasn't prepared to give him up so easily.

He would send for Digby. The man

had his office somewhere in the building, so shouldn't be too hard to track down. 'Bates, take me to my study. Then fetch my lawyer. Have coffee brought to us when he arrives.'

The desk was too high for him to use when sitting in the bath chair. It was high time he resumed his duties as head of this household. This could not be achieved whilst he languished like an invalid. The doctor had told him it would be permissible to start using crutches at the end of the week, so it could hardly do him any harm if he transferred himself to a chair.

This was accomplished easily. Once sitting in his accustomed place, he forgot his annoyance about the dog, the children and their aunt, and turned his mind to more important matters. He wanted to know what had been going on, and had expected to find a pile of unopened correspondence for him to deal with. However, his desk was clear.

Then he recalled he had handed over the reins to Digby. He trusted his man implicitly and was certain nothing untoward had taken place in his absence. In fact, he had never felt so invigorated in his life before — even in the halcyon days when he had had no responsibilities and his older brother and parents had been alive.

The footman carrying the tray arrived at same time as his man of business. Everett was pleased to see Digby had brought his secretary with him, and that the young man was carrying a large wooden box full of documents and papers.

'Good afternoon, your grace, I cannot tell you how delighted I am to see you up and about.' His secretary placed the box on the desktop, and then Digby waved him away.

Both the tray and the box were on the desk, but there was still sufficient room between them to dance a jig if one was so disposed. His lips twitched at the thought that possibly he would be able to do so if his recovery continued.

'Would you be so kind as to pour the coffee, Digby?'

When his lawyer was comfortably seated opposite him, the conversation began. 'I called you here about a trivial thing which is no longer of interest to me. I wish to go through any matters of importance that occurred in my absence from this desk.'

'There is nothing particular to report to you, your grace; everything has been running smoothly as always. The new tenant at Glebe Farm is proving satisfactory, and there have been no reports of vagrants or ex-soldiers encroaching on your land as there have in other neighbourhoods.'

They discussed a variety of things before Digby returned to the original reason he had been summoned. He peered at Everett over the rim of his coffee cup. 'I understand you have met Miss Sinclair and two of your wards. A delightful young lady, and her nieces and nephews are a credit to her. However, your grace, I do not feel it

. . . I wonder if . . . '

'What is it, man? Do not procrastinate.'

'Miss Sinclair has never had the opportunity to mix in society, as she has been looking after those children since she was just out of the schoolroom. Although I believe she intends to appoint a governess to take care of their education, the children are running wild at the moment.'

Everett frowned. This was a contradiction. 'I do not see how she can be taking care of the children as she should if they are running wild.'

'The oldest two can read and write — even the little ones, who are scarcely out of leading strings, can recite the alphabet and count to ten. The aforementioned older children are well-versed in world geography, botany and science, can paint and draw, and are proficient at the pianoforte — at least, Miss Emma is. I'm not exactly clear if they are as good at mathematics as they are at the other subjects.'

'I find that quite extraordinary. If they have no formal lessons, how the devil are they so well-educated?'

'That is a conundrum indeed, your grace. Perhaps when you are mobile again you might visit and discover for yourself?'

'I have every intention of doing so, Digby, and you cannot inveigle me into having them here. The girl was quite clear on that point. They have as little wish to reside here as I have to accommodate them. However, they have acquired my best hound, and I want him returned. It was on that matter that I originally summoned you.'

'If I might be so bold as to make a suggestion, your grace? Why not suggest that they bring him over every day to visit you so you may see that he is flourishing? You might also observe for yourself how the children are doing.'

'I was going to send a body of men over tomorrow to capture the animal, but on further reflection I believe that would be a wasted effort. I find I can move more freely now, and believe I could climb into a gig and drive myself for a visit in a day or two.'

Digby smiled — a rare occurrence, and immediately it roused suspicion. Was there something more to this than he understood?

★　★　★

Lydia half-expected a visitation the following day to try and force the dog to return, but no one appeared from the big house. The children were overjoyed, and quite convinced Benji was now their property. She wasn't so sanguine and felt the matter would not be settled so easily.

Digby had contacted a superior agency in London that supplied domestic staff, governesses, and tutors for the best families in the country. She was now in possession of a handful of applications, four of which seemed possibilities to take charge of the education of her family. Her intention was to invite them down in turn to meet the children. She would not appoint anyone they did not like.

There were still no riding horses in the stable, but she was hoping to rectify that matter once she had dealt with the governess issue. Until then, they must make do with the cob.

She had corralled Emma and Richard, and they had spent a productive few hours at their schoolbooks. They had now left to roam about with the dog, the twins and the nursemaid in tow, under strict instructions to go nowhere near the big house.

This gave her a welcome hour or two in which to continue with her writing. If she continued to write at this pace, her novel would be completed in a matter of weeks. Her method of working involved writing a chapter, doing the necessary edits and changes and then copying it again in a fair hand. This meant that when she wrote the magic words 'The End' there would only be a further week of copying before she was ready to submit it to a publisher.

Her muse was interrupted by a maid with a note. Lydia took the folded paper. Although the writing was unfamiliar to her, she knew the bold, black scrawl could belong to only one person — the duke.

Her fingers trembled as she broke the seal and spread it out on the desk to read.

Miss Sinclair
I have decided that my dog may remain with you at the Dower House for the present. However, I wish to see for myself that he is flourishing; therefore you must present yourself, the dog, and the two oldest children for inspection every day at three o'clock in the afternoon.

She must suppose the indecipherable word at the bottom of this brief letter was his name — Hemingford.

It took half an hour to walk to his house, and the time was after two already. He had deliberately left the delivery of his note so late in order to set her in a panic. There was little chance she would find the children, tidy them up, and be able to get them to him by three o'clock.

Without thinking that it might be considered impertinent, she scribbled a reply on the bottom of the paper.

Your grace
We cannot attend today, but will be with you promptly at three o'clock tomorrow.

She quickly refolded the paper, but was unable to melt the wax as there were no candles alight in the chamber. She would send an outside man with the note, but first she must get Cook to reseal it. The fact that it had her name across the front was immaterial — the person delivering it would be unable to decipher the letters, but well aware to whom he must give it.

The duke might well be displeased

his orders were not being obeyed to the letter, but hopefully he would have recovered his temper by the time they actually went there tomorrow. As her train of thought had been interrupted, she decided not to return to her novel but go in search of the children. She would inform them that they were being allowed to keep Benji as long as they took him to visit his actual owner every day.

As they were forbidden to go in the direction of the big house, they should be relatively easy to locate. They had been discussing the discovery of an abandoned charcoal burner's hut, and she thought it quite likely they with there.

The sun was warm on her face as she strolled along the path that would eventually lead into the wood. She really should have taken the time to put on her bonnet — a well-brought-up young lady would never be seen without her cotton gloves or a bonnet on her head, however hot the weather.

No sooner had she set foot under the welcome shade of the leafy branches than she was greeted by the dog, long pink tongue lolling on the side of his mouth, tail wagging furiously.

'Good afternoon, sir, have you come to lead me to the children?'

In answer, he grabbed her hand and nudged her gently in the direction he had come from. The fact that this would mean she had to negotiate brambles, nettles and hawthorn bushes didn't bother her one jot.

Her skirt was ripped, one arm scratched and the other stung before she arrived at her destination. The children were delighted to see her and unbothered by her disreputable appearance.

'Please say we do not have to return, Aunt Lydia,' Richard said as he danced from one foot to the other in front of her.

'No, not for a while. However, I think the twins had better come back with me, as they have been out of doors long enough and must be ready for a nap.'

Emma poked her head out of the dilapidated hut. 'They left a while ago, Aunt Lydia; they were getting miserable, and David kept complaining he was hungry.'

'I'm not surprised; the picnic you brought with you was hardly enough to sustain you all for a day. I came to tell you some good news.'

* * *

When the message arrived, Everett was unsurprised. He had deliberately sent his note late hoping to agitate the aunt and would have been astonished if they had appeared that day. He supposed he should be affronted by the fact that the girl had scribbled her reply on the bottom of his letter instead of sending him a fresh piece of paper. However, for some inexplicable reason he rather liked her disregard for protocol.

'Bates, I wish to practice with my crutches. Can you find them for me?'

His attendant looked shifty, and immediately he knew the young man had been instructed by the doctor not to give them to him. A few weeks ago he would have roared and shouted and demanded he got his own way, but he was more equable nowadays. Being without pain after five years of misery would make the veriest curmudgeon change his nature. He took pity on Bates. 'When did the doctor say I could have them?'

'The day after tomorrow, your grace. They work a treat, you'll not be disappointed.'

'Excellent news. I was intending to drive myself in the gig as soon as I am more active, but think perhaps that might be overdoing it. I don't suppose you have experience with the ribbons?'

'I can drive the gig, your grace, but couldn't handle a team.'

'In which case, you must find something more appropriate to wear than your livery for when we go out. Ask Mr Digby to arrange it. You have three days, so ensure you are properly equipped by then.'

He sent for the butler and told him to start hiring the extra staff that would be required when the house was fully open. He also asked for his apartment upstairs to be refurbished, redecorated and made ready for his occupation.

'I shall be obliged to hobble about with crutches for a week or two, but then I shall be able to ascend the stairs without difficulty. Will that be sufficient time for you to get things in order?'

Frobisher nodded. 'Ample time, your grace. At the moment there are no females on the staff — do you wish me to appoint a housekeeper?'

'Yes, do that. Leave her to acquire the necessary maids. I intend to entertain as soon as the house is fully opened and everything is as it should be. No doubt there will be more kitchen staff and outside staff required as well. Speak to Mr Digby — I don't wish to be bothered with such trivia.'

Satisfied he had set things in motion,

Everett settled back on the daybed in his sitting room and immersed himself in the newspaper that had arrived that morning. When he retired, he instructed his valet to put out his smartest ensemble. He would be having visitors in the afternoon and wished to make a good impression.

After eating a substantial breakfast, not a meal he usually enjoyed, he sent for Digby. 'It is so long since we entertained here, I've no notion how much time there must be between sending invitations and the event itself.'

'Your grace, what had you in mind? A dinner party? A musical evening? An afternoon garden party?'

'Good God! Nothing so extravagant — I just thought I would invite a few of my nearest neighbours to an informal gathering of some sort.'

'In which case, your grace, invitations must state that the guests are to come for an evening of cards, conversation and supper. Set the time as eight o'clock until midnight.'

'That sounds agreeable to me. When should the cards be sent? I'm having the house opened. Frobisher is acquiring extra staff, and I will be off my crutches in four weeks' time. Therefore, I think this event must take place the second week of July. This will allow five weeks for everything to be made ready satisfactorily.'

'I shall get my secretary to organise the guest list and bring it to show you.'

'That will not be necessary, Digby, I leave the matter to your discretion. I rarely mingle with my neighbours, so one name would be very much like another to me. What would be useful, however, would be some information about the people invited so I'm not in complete ignorance when I meet them.'

'Very well, I shall have that done immediately. Will there be anything else, your grace?'

'One more thing — I don't wish Miss Sinclair or my wards to be without funds. Whatever you are giving her, double it as from today. I can only assume she is dressed so deplorably because she has insufficient funds to improve her wardrobe.'

'With your permission, your grace, I will speak to her myself. I doubt that she will have the names of any suitable seamstresses, and I can supply her with one or two.'

After Digby had left, Everett considered what had been discussed. He was intrigued that an unmarried man of middle years should know the name of even one modiste, let alone two. It was so long since he had spent any time with a female of any description, he found himself eagerly anticipating the visit of Miss Sinclair.

When he had been roistering around Town before the accident, he had avoided any event where he might be pounced on by predatory matrons with insipid daughters on the search for a husband. He had had, of course, a dalliance or two, but always with experienced women of the world.

If he was honest, this young lady was

the first innocent he had had dealings with. Now he was fit, he must think about finding himself a suitable bride, and he could practice his skills on this girl. She was moderately well-bred, reasonably intelligent, and would enjoy being brought into his circle.

She might even be attractive if she was properly dressed. He smiled as he had another idea. He would settle a substantial dowry on her, and make it his business to find her a husband. There must be plenty of gentlemen who would jump at the chance of acquiring a rich bride, even if it meant they would have to take care of his wards until they were old enough to be married off themselves.

6

Mr Digby arrived at the Dower House whilst the older children were busy with their schoolwork and the youngest were practising counting their wooden blocks with their nursemaid.

'Excuse me, children, I must see what the visitor wants. Behave yourselves, I shall be back soon.'

She had half-expected him to come yesterday afternoon, but had been relieved he hadn't. He greeted her with a friendly smile, and her heart stopped banging so hard against her bodice.

'Good morning, my dear Miss Sinclair, I have come with the most wonderful news.'

Somewhat startled by this announcement, she returned his greeting and suggested that they were seated before he continued.

'I shall not stay long, my dear, I have

pressing business elsewhere. His grace keeps me on my toes — I must own that I shall be relieved when he takes full control of his estate again and I can step back.'

'In which case, tell me at once what good news you bring.'

When she heard that the duke had doubled her allowance, she was speechless — not something that occurred often. When she had recovered her composure, she ventured a question. 'I expected him to half it, indeed to — well, I don't know what he might have done after I sent him such an impertinent reply yesterday. Why on earth has he done so?'

'He wishes you to replenish your wardrobe, my dear, and then intends to introduce you into society. I have taken the liberty of sending for a mantua-maker and a milliner. They will attend you tomorrow morning. You must order whatever you want, and clothes for the children too. His grace wishes you all to dress appropriately for your station.'

Lydia glanced down at her somewhat dishevelled appearance. 'I have never been bothered about gowns or bonnets, sir, and have no notion what is *de rigueur* at the moment. I do know that David is supposed to run around in garments meant for a girl, but I could never see the point of that.'

'There is no need for you to worry, my dear girl: Madam Ducracy will bring the latest fashion plates and guide you in your choices. Do not stint, Miss Sinclair, but order as many undergarments, silk stockings, gloves and reticules as you wish.' Her cheeks coloured at his indelicate mention of undergarments, but he continued to smile benevolently at her.

'As I have no intention of attending any parties that require formal attire, I shall restrict myself to morning gowns, promenade gowns and a riding habit. Which reminds me, Digby, I wish to purchase a horse suitable for me, and two ponies for the children.'

'Leave the matter to me, my dear; if I

buy them for you, they need not show up on your accounts. Are you an experienced horsewoman, or do you want something gentle?'

'I love to ride — I used to ride bareback on anything that was available as I was growing up. Sadly, I've had no opportunity to ride at all these past few years. I can use a side-saddle, but prefer to ride astride. Something tall and fast, not small and docile, would suit me best.'

He nodded. 'I'll see what I can do. I understand that you are to take Emma and Richard, plus the dog, to visit his grace this afternoon. How are you intending to achieve that goal, as the dog refused to go near the house last time?'

'I intend to put a leash on him. I know he's quite big enough to pull us over if he so wishes, but I believe that if the children walk on either side of him he will do as we ask.'

'Forgive me for saying so, my dear, but if you have a smarter gown it might be wise to wear it when you go. His grace, I know for a fact, is dressing to impress for your visit.'

She was about to offer a terse reply but reconsidered. If the duke intended to make an effort, then who was she to cavil? 'Thank you for your advice, Mr Digby. I do have one other gown that is slightly less disreputable than this one.'

He took his leave, and she returned to the schoolroom, expecting to find it in chaos — but even the little ones were busy about their tasks.

'You may go and play; you have done very well this morning. Remember, you must be here when you hear the village clock strike two, as you must wash and change before we walk to the big house with Benji.'

'We're not going far today, Aunt Lydia; we're going to give him a bath and make him look ever so smart. We don't want his grace to think we're neglecting his hound,' Emma told her.

'We're coming too,' Lottie pronounced. 'We want to see a duke.'

'Not today, sweetheart; he doesn't like children, and we would not be going ourselves if we weren't ordered to do so.'

'We don't like him either. We're going to help give Benji a bath,' David said, and although Lydia knew this was a bad idea, she didn't have the heart to say no.

It took so long to dry the dog, clean the children, and calm down the twins, that they were tardy with their departure. If they ran, they would arrive hot and flustered, and she had no intention of doing that.

'We must walk briskly, children, and hope we are not disastrously late for our appointment. Shall we sing a song to help us on our way?'

Singing made the journey appear shorter, and the racket kept the dog entertained, so he didn't attempt to slip his lead and hide in the bushes as he had last time.

It would have been sensible to suggest that the children walk in silence for the last hundred yards, but she decided against it. If the duke didn't like what he heard, then that was his concern, not hers.

⋆ ⋆ ⋆

Everett was astonished by the noise coming from the children and their carer as they approached the house. He had been waiting outside the front door to greet them for some considerable time, and as a result, wasn't in the best of humour. As yet, they were unaware they were being watched.

Benji was the first to react to his presence. The dog froze and immediately attempted to run backwards.

'Don't come any closer, he obviously doesn't want to see me!' he yelled. The unexpected shout caused the children to stop in mid-verse, their aunt to stare open-mouthed in his direction, and the dog to sit down.

'Push me towards them, Bates. With luck, my dog won't object if we meet away from the house.'

He was bumped over the drive towards the stationary group, and watched their reaction with interest. The children pressed themselves closer to the dog, who sat with his tail wagging slightly as if he hadn't a care in the world. Miss Sinclair had recovered her composure and was returning his examination in equal measure.

Today she looked slightly more presentable. Her gown was outmoded, but at least it was freshly pressed and relatively clean.

She dipped in a minimal curtsy, the girl did the same, and the boy made an attempt at bowing.

'Thank you for coming. I expected you some time ago. Is there a reason for your tardiness?'

'It is a considerable distance to walk, especially in this hot weather, and I had no wish to distress the children by hurrying.'

This was not the response he was

expecting. However, she had not finished.

'We have come today, your grace, as requested. We shall not be doing so again. You can see he is happy with us. If you wish to see the dog, then you will have to visit us at the Dower House.'

It wasn't often that he was lost for words, but no one had ever had the temerity to address him in this way. She continued to watch him.

Then an extraordinary sound broke the silence. A ferocious growling came from the throat of a dog he'd thought as docile as a donkey. The hound's hackles were up and his teeth were bared. The animal was poised to attack him.

Before Benji sprang, Miss Sinclair ran forward and dropped her hands on the duke's shoulders. 'Look, Benji, we are friends. He means me no harm.'

Everett understood, and forced himself to smile and relax his shoulders. He stretched round and covered one of her hands with his own. 'Silly dog, there's no need to be upset.'

The growling subsided, but the dog still looked tense. If he wasn't careful, matters might get out of hand.

'Children, please take Benji home again. As your aunt has said, I can see my dog has changed allegiance and now belongs to you.'

They didn't need bidding a second time, didn't wait to see if their aunt followed them, but turned around and scampered off, the hound loping beside them. He didn't speak again until the three of them were out of sight.

She had already removed her hands and was now standing beside him. There were tears in her eyes and her lips were trembling.

'I am so sorry, your grace, I'd no idea the dog had become so protective of us. If he had attacked you it would have been my fault.'

'No, the blame was mine. I have a quick temper and take offence easily. Please, Miss Sinclair, will you come inside with me? We need to talk.'

'I should go after the children . . . '

'No, you should not. That dog is more than capable of protecting them. Unless you run, they will be so far ahead of you by now they will be home before you catch them up.'

'You are right, your grace, and it's not as though they haven't been here on their own before. I will come in, but I must not stay long.'

Bates was now pushing him round to the side door through which he was obliged to enter and exit whilst in his chair, and she was walking beside him.

'Good heavens, Miss Sinclair, to stay above fifteen minutes would be a gross breach of etiquette, as we are both aware.'

Her smile changed her face from ordinary to quite beautiful. 'And to be closeted alone with a gentleman to whom one is not related would be even worse in the eyes of the *ton*.'

'We shall converse on the terrace, as I'm quite sure that will break no rules.'

He was at a decided disadvantage

being trundled along like a sack in a barrow, but at that moment he wouldn't change a thing. Bates positioned him by the table as always. Refreshments were already laid out as he had intended to invite them all to remain for tea.

As she brushed past him, he was able to detect the scent of rose and lemon drifting from her shiny tresses.

'As I expected the children to be joining us, you will be unsurprised to discover the refreshments are somewhat unusual.'

She laughed, a lovely natural sound, and one he hoped to hear again. 'Richard and Emma will be disappointed to have missed this feast. Scones, strawberry conserve, a variety of cakes, plus lemonade and buttermilk! All favourites of theirs. I'm sure we shall enjoy the treats ourselves.' She picked up a plate and gestured towards the table. 'What would you like?'

'Whatever you care to give me, my dear. I am unused to eating at this time of day, and can't remember the last time I had a cake or pastry of any sort.'

Bates had politely stepped away, but she beckoned him over. 'I should like coffee, and bring whatever his grace would prefer.'

She gave the order with a natural grace and dignity that surprised him; there was more to this girl than he had first thought.

★　★　★

Lydia's mouth remained unpleasantly dry after the scare Benji had given her. She was certain that if she hadn't prevented it, the animal would have savaged the duke. Was this the sort of dog to be a playmate to her charges?

The last thing she wanted was food, but a glass of lemonade and then a coffee might restore her sufficiently to be able to discuss this matter with the autocratic gentleman beside her.

After carefully splitting two scones and covering them with conserve and cream, she handed him the plate. 'I am going to have lemonade before my coffee — do you wish to have the same?'

'I've not drunk lemonade since I was a boy, but as the coffee has yet to arrive, I will join you in a glass.'

She poured them both a drink and was pleased her hands didn't shake. Then she selected a chair a respectful distance from him, smoothed out the skirt of her gown, and sat down. 'I don't think we should keep Benji after all, however much the children adore him. He was terrifying, and I'm sure he would have attacked you . . . '

'Hounds are bred for their loyalty and fierceness, Miss Sinclair. He was doing his duty — he saw me as a physical threat to your safety and reacted accordingly. I can tell you with absolute certainty that your nieces, nephews and yourself will come to no harm from him. Indeed, you can be sanguine that as long as Benji is with them, they will be safe.'

'That's all very well, your grace, but I've no wish for anyone else to be attacked because the dog believes he is protecting them. I fear the animal is unstable.'

'I'm certain he is not. He has always been a follower, not a leader, and was never completely happy as the under-dog in my pack. He has found his true place in the world, and will be your loyal companion for the next few years.'

'Well, if you are sure that not only the children, but anyone they might meet, will be safe, then I shall say no more about it.'

The coffee arrived and she poured them both a welcome cup of the aromatic, bitter brew. The lemonade and a few sips of this restored her, and she was now ready to indulge in some of the tasty treats set out on the table.

Conversation turned — after discussion about the weather, the price of corn, and other things — to the matter of the children's education.

'I don't believe in confining children

to endless study when the weather is fine. In the winter, it is different, and they are content to work all day at their letters and numbers. I am about to appoint a suitable governess — the interviews begin next week.'

'When I was eight years old, I was sent away to school . . . '

'Richard is staying with me. I don't believe in such practices; I think it cruel and unpleasant for the child concerned.'

His eyes flashed a warning, and she hastily apologised for interrupting him.

'I was not going to suggest that he *did* go away, I was merely telling you what happened to me. You are correct in assuming the experience was unpleasant — I certainly thought so.'

'Good, I'm glad that we can agree on this. I thought that when he is ten years of age, I would appoint a tutor so he could learn things that only a gentleman can teach. Until then, I am content for him to have his lessons with his sister.'

He nodded. 'I agree. I think it necessary to point out to you, Miss Sinclair, that I am the children's legal guardian. You must seek my consent to any changes you wish to make in their daily lives.'

'Let me get this clear, your grace. Although you have no wish to be involved with them in any way, apart from providing the necessary funds for us to live a comfortable life, I need to ask your permission before I make any decisions on their behalf?'

'I don't like children, and don't see the necessity to have them constantly underfoot, but I do accept my responsibilities. I would not be doing my duty if I allowed you to let them run riot all over the country without stepping in to curtail this.'

'I can assure you they are supervised at all times — if not by me, then by a nursemaid. I have asked Mr Digby to purchase them a pony each as I wish them to learn to ride. Does this meet with your approval, your grace?'

'No, it does not. I shall organise this myself. You might not be aware, but I am an expert in horseflesh and run my own stud.'

'I doubt that suitable mounts for my two would be found in such a place. However, if you insist, then I shall leave it to you to inform Mr Digby of the change of plan.' She deliberately didn't mention that his man of business was buying her a hack. She was quite sure that if the task was left to his grace, she would have something quiet and steady — not at all what she required.

The faint echo of the church clock striking four reminded her that she had been with him for almost an hour. Admittedly, they had been sharing a delicious repast, and discussing important issues about the children, but she had overstayed her allotted time by a considerable amount.

'I must go, your grace, and thank you for your hospitality.'

For the first time since she had met him, she thought he might be a gentleman she could like.

'I bid you good afternoon, Miss Sinclair. When I have purchased the ponies, I shall have them sent to you. I take it you have renovated the stabling and appointed grooms to take care of the animals?'

'The matter is in hand, your grace.' She stood up, shook the crumbs from her skirts, and nodded. She wasn't going to continue to curtsy to him as if she were a servant.

She left via the terrace steps, and was about to cut across the grass to the drive when she saw that a smart phaeton was awaiting her arrival.

Two horses, matched chestnuts, looked around at her approach. The coachman bowed. 'His grace said this vehicle is to be at your disposal, miss, if you wish to go anywhere away from the Dower House. You have just to send word to the stables, and I will be there within half an hour.'

'That will be most useful. What is your name? If you are to drive for me I need to know it.'

'I am Jethro, miss. Pleased to be at your service.'

Lydia climbed in unaided and settled back on the comfortable squabs, well-satisfied with her meeting. Having such a smart equipage at her disposal was something she had never thought to attain; it would make her journey to London so much easier.

7

The arrival of the seamstress and her two assistants the following morning was a cause of great excitement. Even the twins were eager to be measured for new garments, and happy to remain reasonably still for the required amount of time. Whilst the assistants and the nursemaid dealt with the children, Madam Ducray devoted her attention to Lydia.

When Lydia spoke to the lady in fluent French, the deception was revealed. 'I beg your pardon, Miss Sinclair; somehow it is thought that the best dressmakers are from Paris, so I adopted a false persona.'

'As long as you are as good at your profession as I've been told, then I care not whether you are French or English.' Lydia picked up the colourful pile of fashion plates. 'Am I to select from these? I do admire the high waist, but I have no wish for flounces, rouleau, ribbons or bows all over my gowns.'

'Very well, miss, I have noted that down. I have swatches of materials here; would you like to choose from the muslins first? These are ideal for daywear. I have silks, satins, organza, sarcenet, and other items which will be ideal for the evening.'

The novelty of selecting patterns, materials and the necessary accoutrements to complement her new ensembles, rapidly faded as the day dragged by. The children were upstairs preparing for bed by the time she was left alone.

She had chosen colours that would complement her dark hair and green eyes. She had no clear idea of what she had ordered, however, as the patterns, materials and adornments blended one into the other after the first few hours. Madam Ducray had strict instructions to complete a riding habit first, as Lydia had every expectation of Mr Digby keeping to his promise and providing her with a riding horse in the next few days.

Although she had done nothing strenuous, she was more than ready to retire at ten o'clock.

'When will your new gowns be ready, miss?' Beth, her newly appointed dresser, asked as she brushed Lydia's hair.

'I didn't think to ask, but I expect the first one will arrive in a day or two. A Miss Fairbrother is coming tomorrow for an interview. Do I have something suitable to wear?'

'I have already sponged and pressed the gown you wore when you visited his grace the other day. Would you like me to arrange your hair differently? If I braid it and put it around your head in a coronet, I believe you will look older.'

'That's an excellent notion, Beth. From the information I garnered about this candidate, Miss Fairbrother is in her thirties, which makes her consider-ably older than I am.'

'Are you sending the pony cart to collect her from the coaching inn?'

'No, I have arranged for the phaeton to do that. It will make a good impression on her. I have already inspected the accommodation she will use if she is appointed, and am satisfied she could have no complaints there.'

'I should think not, miss. All the staff here are ever so well looked after — I doubt even those at the big house do better than we do.'

The next morning, the children had been told to stay close to the house so they could be called in to wash and change an hour before the governess was expected to arrive. Lydia had written out the list of questions she intended to ask, and also a list of rules that whoever was appointed must adhere to. The most important of these was that no physical punishment must be used. She did not believe that beating children did anything to improve their behaviour or temperament.

She intended to make the interview as informal as possible. The candidate was more likely to relax and show her true character when walking about the garden, admiring the house, and avoiding being slobbered on by Benji.

The children had been instructed to behave normally, but not to do anything that would upset Miss Fairbrother. After the informal part of the process, everyone would go inside for refreshments. Then the children could change and run off to play whilst she conducted the interview itself.

The young woman duly arrived, and Lydia took an instant dislike to her. She was supercilious, snapped at the children, and shrieked with horror when the dog came over to investigate. There was no point in continuing the process, and the unsuitable governess was dispatched without the bother of the formal interview.

'You won't appoint her, will you, Aunt Lydia?' Emma asked.

'Of course not, sweetheart, nobody

liked her. I sincerely hope Miss Stevens, who is coming tomorrow morning, will be a better choice. It's impossible to tell a person's character from a letter alone.'

This was not quite true — anyone seeing the duke's handwriting would know at once he was an autocratic aristocrat.

★　★　★

Everett watched the two pretty Exmoor ponies trot by, and nodded. 'They will do. Get a stable lad to ride them before they are taken over to the Dower House. I want to be certain neither animal has any vices.'

He had learned to ride on an Exmoor pony himself, and knew them to be kind, reliable beasts. He would have liked to have visited them in their previous home, but knew them to have been the loving pets of his nearest neighbours' children, and that the family had been reluctant to part with them until now. With luck, they would remain sound for another ten years, allowing the twins to learn to ride on them when they were old enough to do so.

He was hoping there was something in his own stables that would do perfectly for their aunt. He spent the remainder of the morning having his horses paraded in front of him, including anything suitable from his stud.

'No, there's nothing here that will do. Brown, I want a riding horse for Miss Sinclair — nothing too excitable, and not above fifteen hands either.'

His head groom nodded. 'I know of a pretty grey mare for sale — I was thinking of purchasing her to breed from. Shall I have her brought over for you to inspect, your grace?'

'Do that. Do it today. I want the ponies and a mount for Miss Sinclair to be delivered at the same time.'

Satisfied he had done all he could to expedite matters, he got Bates to push him back to his study. He'd approved the guest list he had been shown and the invitations had been sent out. The house was in turmoil, something he would normally have disliked. However, he was rather enjoying seeing the place made ready for visitors.

He was happy to endure the constant racket of labourers, carpenters and suchlike refurbishing and redecorating where necessary. The curtains in the main reception rooms had been removed and sponged, and were in the process of being rehung. Such trivia would not normally interest him, but he was determined to be involved with everything.

An army of journeymen, employed from the local villages, was cleaning windows, pruning hedges, and weeding flowerbeds. He was determined not to have his ancestral home criticised for being in disrepair when his neighbours came to visit for the first time in many years.

Although still forbidden to use his

crutches, so could not see himself upright, he had begun to take an interest in his appearance after many years of neglect. He had had his hair cut short, was clean-shaven, and his eyes were slowly regaining the sparkle they had once had. He was several stones lighter than he had been before the accident, but there was little he could do about that now. Once he was walking again he would do everything he could to improve his stamina and fitness. He was an unmarried duke, and therefore the most desirable bachelor in the country. Nevertheless, when he made his choice he wanted the fortunate young lady to marry him because she found him desirable, not just because of who he was.

He approved the purchase of the grey mare, and arranged for the three animals to be taken to the Dower House the following day. He had no doubt they would be received with delight and he was eagerly anticipating a visit from the children and their carer to thank him for his generosity.

When he saw the phaeton leave for the third day in a row, he was sufficiently intrigued to enquire as to why it was needed so often. Digby came to answer his summons.

'Miss Sinclair is interviewing for a governess for the older children, your grace. Today will be the third and final candidate. Jethro, the coachman, is keeping me fully informed. It seems there was a fourth, but that candidate has withdrawn. So far she has rejected the others, so let us hope this third young lady is considered suitable.'

'I wish I had known this before, Digby, I have sent the ponies and the mare over and they are likely to arrive at the same time as the governess.'

'You have purchased a mount for Miss Sinclair? I thought . . . never mind.'

'Out with it, man. Why are you looking so perturbed?'

'I too have been tasked with finding

Miss Sinclair a hack. The gelding I purchased will also be arriving today.'

'God's teeth! You should have spoken to me before doing so. The gelding will have to be returned from whence it came. I wish her to ride the horse I selected. It will be chaos at the Dower House today.'

'I'm sure Miss Sinclair and the children will be able to deal with whatever occurs, your grace. I have found all of them, including the little ones, exceptionally intelligent.'

Not for the first time, Everett cursed under his breath that he was so incapacitated. He would dearly like to be there to see how the annoying young lady dealt with the arrival of not one, but four equines, plus the prospective governess.

He was damned if he was going to moulder in this bath chair a moment longer. 'Bates, take me inside and then bring me my crutches.'

This time the young man did not prevaricate — a wise decision on his part, as Everett was in no mood to be gainsaid.

He had practised standing on his good leg several times. He had also hopped about the place holding onto the furniture, and was certain he was strong enough to use the crutches, whatever his physician might think about the matter.

With Bates close at hand in case he needed assistance, Everett tucked the objects under his arms. Within a few swings, he had mastered the art, and was able to move freely about the room with no discomfort at all.

'I intend to go to the Dower House at once. Fetch the gig immediately.'

★ ★ ★

'I don't think we need a governess, Aunt Lydia,' Emma said as they were eating breakfast.

'I know the other candidates were not right, my love, but Miss Carstairs sounds ideal. Remember not to go far, as you will have to come in and get ready mid-morning.'

The twins ate in the nursery, as they were not old enough to sit at the table with the adults. The older children took breakfast and midday refreshments with their aunt in the dining room, but she dined alone in the evening and the children had nursery tea upstairs.

Yesterday's interview had barely lasted half an hour as the applicant had turned out to be myopic and very deaf — hardly a suitable person to take care of these children. Lydia read through the letter Miss Carstairs had sent. The young lady had worked for three years with a well-to-do family who resided in Bath. She had only left because her employers had decided to move to their northern estates, and Miss Carstairs had no desire to follow them.

Her references were glowing, and Lydia had a strong feeling this final candidate would be a perfect match for her charges. The governess stated her academic qualifications — which were exemplary — and also mentioned having a love for animals and the outdoors, plus that she would welcome the opportunity to accompany the children if they rode out.

Benji had taken up residence in the entrance hall. He now had a rug positioned in the far corner where he stretched out every night to sleep. The dog made no attempt to come upstairs, and neither did he venture into the other reception rooms on the ground floor.

Although his accommodation should be outside in the yard, Lydia rather liked the fact that such a large beast was prowling around downstairs making sure there were no unwanted visitors during the night. Her staff had been talking about the spate of burglaries taking place at other houses in the neighbourhood — this was being blamed on disaffected ex-soldiers who had returned from the Peninsular War and were now without gainful employment.

The first of her new gowns had arrived early that morning by carrier, and she decided to change into it. She had never owned anything as elegant, and it would do no harm to appear dressed fashionably for a change.

She heard the children go past as she was getting into her new ensemble. 'I don't want my hair in a coronet, it is an uncomfortable style. Just do it in my normal manner, please, Beth.'

'There, miss, you look a picture. Forget-me-not blue is perfect with your colouring, although green would be better as it matches your eyes.' Her maid adjusted the neckline, fiddled with the sash in a darker shade of blue, and Lydia was ready.

The gown had puffed sleeves edged with the same blue satin of the sash, but that was the only extra decoration. 'How different I feel wearing a fashionable gown. Having the waist under one's bosom is rather odd, but extremely comfortable.'

'Are you going to wear the gloves and

bonnet, miss, as you intend to walk about outside?'

Lydia was about to refuse, but then reconsidered. 'I believe I shall — after all, I have matching slippers, and it would be a shame not to wear the entire ensemble.'

By the time she was ready, the children were clattering downstairs again, and she heard the crunch of carriage wheels in the turning circle outside.

'I must hurry; I shall be tardy, and that would not be an auspicious start to the interview. I cannot expect my employee to be punctual if I do not do the same myself.'

As she arrived in the hall, she received a message to go around to the stable yard immediately. She was inappropriately dressed for such a visit, but had no option.

It was quicker to exit the house by the side door and take the flagged path which led directly to the stables. The sound of children shrieking in the distance made her increase her steps. She emerged through the brick arch and almost fell over her feet at what she saw.

'Good morning, Miss Sinclair. Forgive me for arriving unannounced, but I wished to present the children with their ponies myself.'

She remained rooted to the spot, unable to make a sensible response. He was very tall, not something she had been aware of until now. To see him standing, albeit with the help of crutches, was a shock indeed.

'Good morning, your grace. I am indeed surprised to see you. Benji is not here to greet you; I expect he fears you intend to take him away.' She was gabbling, not making conversation, but if she was not to seem a complete ninny she must gather her wits immediately. 'Where are the ponies?'

'They are in the meadow with the children. Before you go and see them, Miss Sinclair, I would like you to inspect another arrival in your yard.' He pointed towards a loose box which had been unoccupied until that morning. Now the sounds of a horse inside were quite evident.

Forgetting she was dressed in a gown that did not belong in a stable yard, she ran across and leaned over the half-door. Inside was the prettiest little grey mare, an ideal mount for a timid rider — but not at all suitable for her.

Then he was beside her, his shoulder too close to hers. 'Her name is Peggy. I thought her ideal for you.'

'Thank you, your grace, it was kind of you to think of us like this. Indeed, we are honoured by the fact you have come in person to present your gifts.' She was unaccountably flustered by his proximity and stepped away. 'Forgive me, sir, but I am expecting the arrival of someone who has applied for the position of governess. I believe I heard the phaeton arriving.'

Not waiting for his response, she picked up her skirts and fled. As she had thought, a young lady was at that very moment descending from the carriage. Miss Carstairs was of medium build and average height, but no one would forget her. The young lady's hair was quite visible under her bonnet. It was the most extraordinary colour, a startling shade of red.

★   ★   ★

Everett deftly turned so he could lean his elbows on the half-open stable door and watch the girl run away. There was something different about her today, but he couldn't think what it might be. He had a choice to make — should he join the children or follow their aunt?

Curiosity got the better of him. Bates, who had acted as his driver, was hovering about as if expecting his master to sprawl on his face at any moment. 'Don't bother to unharness the team, I won't be above a quarter of an hour.'

He could move swiftly on his

crutches and arrived at the turning circle in front of the house only moments after the girl. Devil take it! His noisy arrival had alerted them, and they had turned to watch him. He had no alternative but to approach when all he had intended to do was observe from the shadows.

When he arrived at their side he waited to be introduced, and there was an awkward moment when they all stood in silence.

'Your grace, how kind of you to join us so unexpectedly. Allow me to introduce you to Miss Carstairs, who will be coming here as the children's governess.'

Whether he or the young lady herself were the more surprised by this announcement, it was hard to tell. What was Miss Sinclair thinking? She could hardly have made an informed decision after an acquaintance of barely a minute?

'Come along, Miss Carstairs, I must take you to the children you will be teaching. His grace has kindly purchased them Exmoor ponies which have only just arrived.'

Both young ladies curtsied politely and then strolled off as if he was of no importance. His first impulse was to throw one of his crutches after them, but he restrained himself. As they vanished into the house, he finally understood what had been bothering him about Miss Sinclair's appearance.

Today, she looked like a young lady of quality — which she was — and no longer like a poor relation. His determination to find her an accommodating husband was strengthened by this change. He would discuss the matter with Digby, as his man would most probably know of a suitable candidate in the neighbourhood.

The man must be reasonably attractive, not more than ten years her senior, and preferably a man with little expectations of his own. He needed to be certain that whoever the girl married would not suddenly take the bit between his teeth and foist the brats on him. He would have to make it very clear that although they were his legal responsibility, he had no intention of allowing them to live with him.

He was about to make his way to the yard where his carriage was waiting when the little ones emerged from the front door, his erstwhile dog at their side. Benji ignored him and the children and their nursemaid appeared unaware he was watching them.

The children had a ball made from rags and they took it in turns to throw it. He hadn't been aware that the hound would retrieve, but the dog trotted the necessary few yards, picked up the object in his mouth and carried it back to carefully place it at the feet of whichever child had thrown it.

He was entranced and remained leaning against the wall in the shadows for far longer than he had intended. Reluctantly he made his way to his carriage and clambered in. 'Home, Bates, I am redundant here.'

On his return, he had no need to send for Digby as the man was waiting for him in the study. 'Everybody we sent an invitation to, your grace, has replied in the affirmative. This means there will be fifty guests attending. I thought, as there are so many to entertain, perhaps you would like me to engage some musicians.'

'Whatever you think best, Digby; the matter is entirely in your hands. As long as there are cards, a decent supper, and good conversation, then I shall be content. Before you go, there's another matter I wish to discuss with you.'

He explained his plans for the children's aunt, and Digby nodded. 'An excellent notion, your grace, and one I applaud. No young lady should remain a spinster with no children of her own. I have several gentlemen in mind — do I have your permission to add them to the invitation list? Which reminds me, an invitation was not sent to Miss Sinclair; I shall rectify that omission immediately.'

'Excellent. You will no doubt have noticed I am now upright and able to get about the place without that wretched chair. By the time my neighbours come, I will be whole again and ready to face the world once more.'

'This great house is beginning to look as it used to, your grace, and I can assure you that the dozens of new staff that have been appointed are all delighted to be here.'

'So I should hope. These past five years have been difficult for me personally, but I pride myself on having remained a good landlord and employer. If this affair is successful, then I wish to invite old friends and family for a house party. I believe I should enjoy having people staying here for a few weeks.'

'Exactly when did you have in mind, your grace? People require at least a month's notice if they are to be away from home for an extended period. Your supper party will be the most talked-about event held in the neigh-bourhood this year — I'm sure you are aware that any event held here is guaranteed to be successful. Therefore, your grace, I think you should begin to consider those you wish to invite to your house party. August would be ideal — July would be too early, and September too late.'

Everett raised an eyebrow. This was the longest speech he'd ever heard his man of business utter. What had made the man so garrulous?

'I will have the names for you by the end of the week. Miss Sinclair has appointed a governess, and I wish you to visit to see that she has made a sensible choice. I must own that I'm beginning to warm to my wards. They are a trifle unruly, but intelligent and well-behaved despite that.'

'They are a delightful family, your grace; and the more you see of them, the better you will like them.'

His man of business hurried off to add people to the invitation list. Miss

Sinclair was no simpleton: Everett knew he must be subtle with his plans for her future, or she would find him out and put a stop to it.

* * *

Lydia hoped she didn't regret her spontaneous decision to appoint Miss Carstairs before the children had made her acquaintance. The young lady in question was equally puzzled by this impulsive behaviour.

'Miss Sinclair, I understood my appointment depended on the approval of the children I am to take charge of, and yet you have told his grace I have the position.'

'I'm sure they will both like you, and I apologise for speaking so intemperately. The duke is the children's guardian, and I live in fear of him deciding to take them away from me. So far, he has shown little interest in their well-being apart from supplying us with a very generous income.'

'I appreciate that, but it doesn't explain why you felt the need to offer me the job in such a precipitate fashion.'

'I have no other candidates coming — you were the last of the applicants that I invited for interview . . . ' Lydia stopped, appalled at what she had been about to say. 'The first two candidates were completely unsuitable, but I knew as soon as I saw you stepping down from the carriage that you would be perfect. I deliberately left your interview until the last for that reason.'

The governess shook her head. 'So you didn't offer the post to me as you had no other choice?'

'No, of course I didn't. You see, my dear, I wished to be sure you were the right candidate by seeing the other two as well. If I had seen you first, then I would have appointed you immediately and cancelled the other visits.'

Miss Carstairs laughed. 'Now it is clear to me, Miss Sinclair. You have done exactly as I would have in similar circumstances. All that remains is for me to meet the children and get their approval.'

'They are with their ponies at the moment, so I will show you around first and allow them to enjoy this special morning. I know what will make it certain they wish you to stay — if you offer to teach them to ride as part of their curriculum. I was intending to do so myself, but I see no reason why you shouldn't do it in my stead.'

'There's nothing I should like better. Do you have a mount that I can use so I can take them out once they are proficient?'

'His grace sent a beautiful grey mare for that very purpose. My own horse is arriving later today, so we shall be able to ride together.'

Miss Carstairs announced herself delighted with everything she saw, including her own accommodation. Lydia had not put her on the nursery floor but given her a pretty apartment on the family floor.

Emma and Richard were as enthusiastic about the arrival as she was. Their new governess departed to collect her belongings, and promised to be with them the next day.

'I shall excuse you your schoolwork today, children, as you will have a more regular routine once Miss Carstairs is established here. You will do your studies in the mornings in the schoolroom and, if the weather is clement, you will have outside activities in the afternoons. You will work on Saturday morning, but have Saturday afternoon and Sunday free — apart from attending church, of course.'

They rushed upstairs to change out of their best and into something they could get dirty without fear of being chastised. She did the same, as she wished to put on her riding habit and take her own horse out for a hack as soon as he arrived.

She had been hoping her new outfit would have arrived before the horse, but unfortunately this was not the case.

Therefore, she would have to make do with the habit she had used many years ago when she was still a girl. She was shocked to see the hem was a good three inches from her ankles, and the jacket would barely close at the front. There was nothing she could do about this — she would be wearing riding boots, and they would ensure there was no indecent exposure of stockings, despite the shortness of the skirts. There was little she could do about the tightness of the bodice, and she would just have to pray the buttons did not give way whilst she was riding.

The children had wandered off with Benji and were no longer with the ponies. The head groom, Sam, greeted her with a smile. 'I turned out the little mare, Miss Sinclair; I find that horses which are kept outside do better than the animals confined to stables.'

'I agree, but in the winter my horse and the mare will need to be inside, even if the ponies and the cob remain out.'

A large brown head hung over the loose box door, and she hurried over to greet the new arrival. 'What is his name?'

'Sydney, miss; don't answer to anything else, so I'm told.'

She pulled the animal's ears affectionately, and the gelding snuffled and rubbed his velvety lips on her shoulder. 'Well, Sydney, you are a fine fellow indeed. I see that you're ready to go out, so shall we proceed?'

She unlatched the door and grasped his bit. He emerged from the box without fuss. Sam hoisted her into the saddle, and waited whilst she adjusted her position and put her foot into the single stirrup iron.

'He's a big horse, miss, but as far as I can tell has no vices and a soft mouth. Do you want me to come out with you?'

'As we don't have another riding horse available, you couldn't come even if I wished you to. However, I don't intend to do more than ride around the adjacent lanes, and perhaps have a collected canter through the woods. I wish to get to know him before I venture further. As the duke owns all the land within a five-mile radius of here, I don't think I will be offending anyone if I ride alone.'

For the first mile, Lydia kept the gelding to a sedate walk, as she had no wish to go any faster until she had the measure of her mount. 'I am going to like you, Sydney, despite your unfortunate name. Shall we trot?'

She applied a little pressure to his flank and he instantly responded. Within a few strides, she had settled into the rhythm, and revelled in the experience of riding a spirited horse. Once she was confident she was in full control, she settled back into the saddle, shortened her reins, and pressed harder with her heel.

Again he did as he was asked, breaking into a collected canter. As she was unfamiliar with the route, she thought it better not to urge him to go faster. She realised after a mile or two that she was perilously close to the big house — she was catching glimpses of this edifice through the trees. She had no wish to appear unexpectedly in the duke's park, so decided it might be better to retrace her path.

'That's enough, Sydney; trot now, there's a good fellow.' She leaned back a little and applied gentle pressure to the reins, delighted her mount accepted her instructions so readily.

Once they were walking, she began the tricky manoeuvre of turning him on the narrow path. This involved shortening the inside rein and pressing firmly with her heel. They were halfway around when he stopped and snorted, tossing his head and becoming agitated.

'What's wrong? Sydney, stand still whilst I take a look.'

She twisted in the saddle, resting one hand on his rump so she could see into the thick shrubbery his hindquarters were standing in. She saw at once what the problem was — he had become entangled in a bramble patch, and there was no way he could extricate himself without assistance.

She would have to dismount and release him herself. Getting down would be no problem; however, he was so tall there was no way she could scramble back into the saddle unless she could find something to stand on.

She patted the horse's neck, and he tossed his head as if understanding she was going to help him. The ground was soft and her booted feet landed without making a sound. Unless she was careful, she could find herself similarly stuck in the briars. A riding habit had a voluminous skirt, and wasn't meant for the wearer to wander about on the ground.

She didn't know her mount well enough to be certain he would remain stationary when she released his reins, but if she held onto them she wouldn't be able to remove the brambles from his legs.

'Stand, Sydney, stand.'

She kept her hand resting against him as she moved to his hindquarters. She would have to be careful as the thorns were sharp, and if they dug into the horse he would likely bolt. She kept talking to him softly as she worked, and he remained calm and relaxed, occasionally turning his head and giving her a gentle shove in the back. It took far longer than she'd anticipated to release him, but eventually she succeeded.

'There, my boy, you are free of brambles.' She returned to his head and patted his neck. He nuzzled her, leaving a trail of slobber on her shoulder.

'Now, Sydney, we must find somewhere I can remount as I've no wish to walk all the way back to the Dower House.'

The noise of the stable yard at Hemingford Court indicated she was within a quarter of a mile from the building. She had no alternative but to make her way there, and either make use of the mounting block or ask a groom to give her a leg-up to the saddle.

She had already pulled the reins over the gelding's ears to make leading him an easier task, and the massive horse appeared content to amble along beside her listening to her chatter. The path she was on divided, and she took the one that went in the direction of the stables. To her consternation it didn't emerge at the rear of the house, but onto the immaculate lawn that surrounded Hemingford.

All might have been well if the two hounds belonging to the duke had not seen her from the terrace and bounded towards her. She knew they were friendly animals and meant them no harm, but Sydney viewed their approach quite differently.

He threw his head up in horror, lifting her from the ground, and she had no time to release the reins before he took off at a gallop. She was flung headlong onto the grass, and for a few agonising moments she was unable to breathe.

8

Everett had seen the girl, leading a massive gelding, emerge from the woods at the same moment that his dogs had. He cursed the slowness of his reaction as he failed to stop them running headlong to greet the unexpected arrival.

He watched the horse react and saw the girl being thrown to the ground. Without conscious thought, he negotiated the terrace steps, and began swinging across the grass towards the fallen rider.

Miss Sinclair was making hideous gasping sounds. His panic subsided. She was winded — painful, but not serious. His dogs were nosing at the girl, whining and wagging their tails. The gelding, having recovered from his fright, had turned and was trotting back towards his fallen rider.

'Stay where you are, my dear, take deep breaths. Don't try to move until you are fully recovered.'

He couldn't drop down to the grass beside her, couldn't check she had no broken limbs or other injuries. He was about to yell for someone to come from the house when his head groom came rushing from the stable yard, and moments later the housekeeper and Digby were running to join them.

Simpson crouched down and expertly ran her hands along the girl's limbs. 'I'm sure there is nothing broken. You can turn over now, Miss Sinclair, and I will assist you to your feet.'

There was a muffled reply which he couldn't hear. His housekeeper sat back, her cheeks pink. There was something untoward going on.

'Miss Sinclair, are you injured in some way that we cannot see?' He received no answer from the girl, but his housekeeper replied, 'Your grace, please could I request that you, and the other gentlemen, leave this matter to myself and Miss Sinclair to deal with?'

He wasn't to be fobbed off so easily. 'What the devil is going on?'

Finally, the girl spoke. 'Go away, I am in an embarrassing position. The bodice of my habit has torn.'

'I beg your pardon. I should have realised why you were not turning around.' He wasn't sure whether he was uncomfortable or amused by the situation. He snapped his fingers and the other men went as quickly as they had arrived.

He had become adept at balancing on one leg and with the aid of his crutch under his armpit, he managed to remove his jacket. 'Here, Simpson, use this. Bring Miss Sinclair into the house so that she may rectify her garment.'

He had no intention of leaving, but merely turned his back on the two of them.

After a few minutes of whispered conversation, the girl spoke to him. 'You can turn now, your grace, I am no longer in danger of embarrassing you.' He turned, and to his surprise she was smiling. 'Thank you for giving me this; now, instead of exposing my undergarments, I am a figure of fun.'

The sleeves of his topcoat were so long that her hands were invisible, and the silver buttons ensured that her bosom was safely covered.

'You are taller than I realised, my dear, and your . . . ' He stopped; he had been about to say something indelicate about her breasts.

Instead of being offended, she laughed out loud. 'I knew when I put this on that it was somewhat tighter than when I had worn it five years ago. No doubt you have also noticed the skirts are several inches above my ankles.'

He glanced down. 'Now that you mention it, my dear, I can see that your habit has been outgrown. I hope you have ordered another one to be made for you?'

For some reason, the housekeeper

had moved away, leaving them to talk alone. Probably a good thing in the circumstances, as their conversation was highly unsuitable.

'I have indeed, your grace; thanks to your generosity, we shall all be impeccably dressed and in the height of fashion.' She stepped away and started to walk towards the house.

He, in his shirtsleeves and waistcoat, hopped beside her. The top of her head came just above his shoulder — a perfect height for a young lady, in his opinion.

He had quite forgotten about her horse, but the animal had not forgotten about them. Suddenly the gelding's huge head insinuated itself between them as if wishing to join in with the conversation.

'Sydney, I hope you are ashamed of yourself! See how friendly the dogs are? They are nothing to get flustered about.'

The hounds were trotting along beside the horse as if they belonged there. 'Why are you riding this animal when I gave you a far more suitable mount this morning?'

'The mare will be ideal for the governess to use when she takes Richard and Emma out once they have mastered the ability to ride. Mr Digby had already set in motion the purchase of something more to my liking.'

'If you had been riding the mare, my dear, this nonsense would not have occurred, as you would have been able to remount without difficulty. In future, I insist that you always take a groom with you.'

He expected her to disagree, to argue with him, but instead she nodded. 'You are right on both counts, your grace, but unfortunately I have nothing in my stables suitable for my groom to ride. I take it you intend to give me another horse so I can follow your sensible instructions?'

'Devil take it! That will make two horses, two ponies, my prize hound, plus the exclusive use of my phaeton and chestnuts. Is there anything else you intend to take from me?'

Her laugh sent a strange tingle down his spine. 'Well, your grace, one might say I have already taken the coat from your back.'

He stepped aside to allow her to enter the house before him. 'I knew the moment I set eyes on you, my dear, you were going to be trouble.'

'I'm always happy to oblige, your grace . . . '

Something strange was happening to him, and to his astonishment he found himself laughing. Something he had not done since his accident.

'If you are obliging, my dear, then I am the devil incarnate.'

'Many a true word is spoken in jest, sir.'

The housekeeper was waiting politely at the bottom of the stairs, and she walked gracefully over to join her. How the girl still managed to look so feminine when draped in his jacket, he had no idea. He made his way to his own apartment and his valet restored his appearance.

When he returned, he was informed that his guest had already departed. She had decided to borrow a jacket from one of his footmen, and without a second thought had cantered off on her horse.

★   ★   ★

Lydia felt somewhat conspicuous in her gold-frogged green jacket — but at least she was decently covered. The stable boy who took Sydney from her had more sense than to comment on her unusual appearance.

'Turn him out with the others — he will do better in the paddock than cooped up in the stable, especially when the weather is so warm. I shall not be able to exercise him until my new habit arrives from the seamstress.' There was no necessity for her to have provided this information, especially to a stable lad, but she was not the sort of person who treated her staff as inferior beings — unlike someone she knew who lived not far away.

She had been gone for hours, had missed nursery tea, and the children would be wondering what had become of her. Before she went up to see them, she must change out of the ruined habit and put her muslin gown back on.

Beth was not so reticent as the stable lad when she saw her mistress. 'Goodness me, miss, whatever next! I've never seen the like.'

Lydia laughed. 'I know, I look bizarre. I shouldn't have ventured forth in my old habit, and shall not do so again. This can go to someone smaller than I am — I'm sure there must be a young lady somewhere who would appreciate it.'

'I doubt it; young ladies who are happy to take used garments do not usually have a horse to ride.' The girl held up the voluminous skirt. 'There's a lot of good material here: I'm sure this can be made into something else. Shall

I put it in the charity box?'

'Do that for me. Thank you.' She sniffed her hands and pulled a face. 'I really should have a strip wash — I shall scrub my hands and face for now, and that will have to do until I retire. Please ensure there is ample hot water up here for me when I come up.'

The children greeted her with squeals of excitement. The twins were already in their nightgowns and looked ready for bed. Richard and Emma were still dressed and playing quietly on the rug.

'I apologise for being so tardy, my loves, I had an unfortunate experience at Hemingford. Would you like to hear about it?'

By the time she had finished her amusing story the little ones were asleep. She picked up Lottie and the nursemaid collected David — together they carried them into the freshly painted bedchamber they shared.

When she returned, she invited the older two to accompany her outside so they could meet her equine companion.

'He's very big, Aunt Lydia,' Richard said as he clambered onto the fence to view the gelding.

'As I explained to you earlier, my love, that is why I had no option but to try and find a mounting block.'

Sydney, on hearing her voice, pricked his ears and trotted across to greet her. She was strangely touched by his actions, as she had only known him for a few short hours.

The ponies had no intention of being left out of this occasion, and charged across for their share of patting and affection.

'Miss Carstairs and I will teach you both to ride. I hope that your habit comes tomorrow, Emma, otherwise you will have to postpone that treat.'

'I shall put on Richard's breeches, and then I can ride like him and not be obliged to wait.'

'You will do no such thing, young lady. His grace has sent you a lovely side-saddle, and you will learn to ride with that.'

The girl pulled a face, but didn't argue further. They had a pleasant stroll around the garden as the light faded, and then she took them upstairs to supervise their bedtime rituals.

Her supper was waiting on the table in her sitting room and she devoured it hungrily. When she was replete, and the tray quite empty, she wandered into her bedroom and was delighted to find that Beth had not just provided hot water, but also filled the hip bath so she could have a total immersion.

Miss Carstairs arrived the next day as promised, and Lydia was pleased to see her. 'I don't expect you to take up your duties today — spend the time getting to know your surroundings. I told Richard and Emma that they would be doing formal schoolwork in the mornings, and be outside for botany or physical activities in the afternoons.'

'That is exactly what I plan to do, Miss Sinclair. I have drawn up a curriculum for the older children which I would like you to see before I begin tomorrow. Although the twins are too young to be in the schoolroom, I noticed that they like to be with their older siblings, so am happy to have them for an hour or two, and will start teaching them their letters.'

'Thank you, they will enjoy that. They are all very bright, and I believe quite advanced for their years. I do not hold with the theory that children should be seen and not heard, and soundly disciplined for the slightest infraction. Kindness and compassion are far better teachers.'

She left the governess to oversee the unpacking of her trunk and valise. Lydia had appointed one of the new girls to be her dresser — an unusual thing to do, but she wanted Miss Carstairs to become part of the family, and therefore intended to treat her in the same way she would a relation.

The children had been given the day off, so the house was empty. She hurried to the study and settled down to a quiet hour or two of writing; she was so near the conclusion of her book that every moment she spent away from her characters was a torment.

A letter arrived from Mr Digby, but she tossed it to one side to read when she had finished writing this penultimate chapter.

The next few days passed in a flurry of activity as the children began their new regime with the governess and Lydia finished copying the final chapter of her novel. Her new habit had arrived; she had been out on Sydney every day since, and the more she rode him the better she liked the gelding.

Miss Carstairs, who she now called by her given name of Viola, was more like a sister than an employee. The riding lessons were progressing well, and both children were now able to guide their ponies without a leading rein.

Dinner was served to both Viola and herself in the dining room after the children had gone up. Lydia felt quite daring eating so late, but as they all took refreshments at midday, she wasn't ready for dinner until seven o'clock at the earliest.

'The children can now walk, trot, and canter safely. The ponies are impeccably trained and stop if told to. I think they are ready to go for a gentle hack with me accompanying them on the mare.'

'Then take them, Viola, but I shall not accompany you as I don't think having Sydney towering over them would improve their confidence.'

'I noticed that you have ridden the other horse that arrived from his grace's stable — do you prefer him to your own mount?'

'No, he has a hard mouth and is less amenable. He is for the groom to ride when I start going further afield on my hacks.' She put down her cutlery and wiped her mouth on the napkin. 'Which brings me to another subject entirely. I received an invitation to attend a party at the big house the day that you arrived, but have not yet replied. I wonder if you would consider coming with me, as I shall know no one there, and would feel far more comfortable with you beside me.'

'I should love to come, but I cannot. Firstly, because I do not have an invitation; and secondly, because I do not have a suitable evening gown for such a prestigious occasion.'

'Fiddlesticks to that, my dear. I have a wardrobe full of beautiful gowns, and I'm sure that at least one of them will be perfect on you. We are of similar build and height — it's only our colouring that is so different. As to the lack of invitation, if you're willing to come then I shall send a note to Mr Digby to include you on the list.'

The matter settled, they talked of other things. 'I have been hearing that Hemingford Court has been completely refurbished over the past few weeks. The duke became a recluse after his accident, you know, and let the house fall into disrepair. Since the advent of the new physician, who was able to reset his injured leg so he can walk, both the house and the grounds are looking spectacular.'

'From what you have told me, Lydia, the gentleman in question had every right to be curmudgeonly. Indeed, I think you have the best of the bargain by being allowed to remain here in sole control of the children, with a magnificent allowance, and practically no interference from him at all.'

'I thank God for it every day. Until we came here, we had nothing — no servants, little to eat, and we lived in a dilapidated and dreary house. His grace has been so generous, I cannot fault him for that. I think, given time, he will come to love the children as I do, but I'm in no hurry to promote this interaction, as it might mean he wishes us all to move to Hemingford.'

'You should be pleased if you were asked to, Lydia. You are an attractive young lady and should be out and about in society, not mouldering away here bringing up someone else's children.'

'I have no wish to marry anyone, so have no need to socialise. I am a novelist and my first book is complete. I shall find myself a publisher in the next week or two. The duke's largesse has made it possible for me to pay for publication — I have no need of an advance — but I am hoping I will find a company who loves my work as much as I do, and is willing to pay me for the privilege of bringing it out.'

'The children told me that you were writing a book, but I had no idea it was ready for publication. It is not the done thing for a lady to write for a living; do you intend to use a pseudonym?'

'No, I am proud of my writing. This is another reason I have no wish to wed as a husband would have complete control of my finances and my life. At the moment, I am independent . . . '

'Forgive me for saying so, but your independence is reliant entirely on the generosity of the children's guardian. Do not you think it might be wise to disguise your name? From what I've learned of the duke, he is a stickler for the rules. I think he might react badly if you became the centre of unpleasant gossip.'

'This is another reason I wish to be paid for what I do, as then I won't be beholden to anyone. If he decides to remove the children from my care and send me about my business, then so be it. I'm sure you understand it's essential for me to build my reputation as a writer, so I can support myself if needs be.'

Her friend remained unconvinced. 'In my opinion, Lydia, you should find yourself a doting husband who will allow you to do whatever you please. An older man, with deep pockets and no desire to fill his nursery, would be ideal for you.'

Strangely, at these words, an image of the duke's dark features filled Lydia's head.

9

'Am I making the kind of progress you expected? Will I be a whole man again?' Everett asked the doctor.

'Your leg should function as it used to, your grace. I suggest that you use your crutches initially, and just put weight on your leg occasionally until you have become accustomed to using it.'

'The party is in four days' time. I intend to be walking normally by then.'

'You should be walking normally by tomorrow. I'm looking forward to the event — it's a long time since I attended anything of the kind.'

'I can scarcely recall the names of most of the people I invited as it's so long since I mingled with my neighbours. Digby has assured me all the necessary people have been included, and after the party I expect to be in circulation once more. I must thank you for making this possible. I owe you a debt of gratitude I can never repay.'

'I have been well paid for my services, your grace, and seeing you back on your feet is reward enough. I became a physician to help people — you do not owe me anything more.'

'Once my guests see my miraculous recovery, you will be inundated with requests for your services.'

'I am already oversubscribed, your grace, as word of my work has travelled around the vicinity already. I have taken on an assistant, an apothecary, who in future will deal with the minor cases, leaving me free to deal with anything major.'

The doctor departed satisfied that his handiwork was successful. Everett had used his injured leg several times already, and decided to abandon his crutches immediately and not wait until the next day.

Bates hovered anxiously in case he was needed. The young man had become part of his life, and he intended to keep him on even though he already had a perfectly good valet. There were always messages to be run, things to be fetched and Bates would be ideal for this purpose.

'In future you will not wear livery, Bates, but dress as my personal assistant. Digby will take care of this.'

He handed his crutches over and received his ivory cane in return. He had no wish to damage his repaired leg by overdoing it too soon — using his stick was a sensible precaution but one he would abandon before the party.

Walking was no longer agony, and with every step he took he became more confident. After half an hour, he was certain his leg was sound. He was cured. Tonight he would sleep in the correct place for the first time in his life. The master suite had been unoccupied since his father had died, and he was eager to see his new domain.

'Come with me, Bates, I'm going to

inspect my chambers. Then I intend to ride. I wish you to accompany me — I take it you can ride?'

'I can, your grace; my pa was an ostler at the Red Lion.'

That afternoon, Everett was astride his beloved stallion Othello, and Bates was mounted on a bay. Somehow the young man had acquired suitable garments, and now looked as he should.

'I'm going to ride over to the Dower House. You will wait with the horses whilst I am there. I doubt I shall be more than half an hour.'

This time he cantered down to the drive that led to his destination and didn't take the path through the woods. He wished for his arrival to be seen.

Benji bounded out of the shrubbery and hurtled towards him. The dog had the sense to slow his speed before he collided with Othello. His stallion was familiar with the hound, and the sudden arrival didn't spook him. 'Good afternoon, I'm pleased to see you too, my boy. You are looking well — living here obviously suits you.'

The dog stretched up his head and licked Everett's gloved hand. If the dog was out here, then the older children could not be far away. Sure enough, their voices echoed through the trees, and then they ran towards him.

His stallion was unfamiliar with children and might take exception to them. He could not risk either of them being hurt so he kicked his feet from the stirrups and swung to the ground. Instinctively he braced himself for the agony he had always felt when his damaged leg hit the ground — but he landed smoothly and with no pain at all.

He didn't have to ask Bates to take his horse, the young man was already dismounted and was ready to take the reins.

He walked towards the running children and was mystified when they skidded to a halt, and stared at him open-mouthed.

'You can walk, sir, we didn't know you could do that,' the boy said.

'I can indeed, and intend to do so at every possible opportunity. I have come to speak to your aunt — is she receiving this afternoon?'

'Receiving what? I think all our new clothes have arrived,' the boy said.

The girl pushed her brother sending him sprawling. 'You are so stupid, Richard. His grace means, is Aunt Lydia ready to speak to any visitors.'

'That was poorly done of you, young lady. Help your brother to his feet and apologise immediately.' He had not intended to intervene but he could not let such bad behaviour go unchecked.

The girl turned pale, curtsied, grabbed her brother and muttered an apology. The two of them shuffled backwards, no longer comfortable in his company. Then they turned and fled — the dog growled at him and then raced after them.

'What the devil was that all about?'

'Forgive me for saying so, your grace,

but I don't reckon they've ever been spoken to so sharply by a gentleman like you. Fair scared them half to death.'

'I'd no wish to frighten them, but I'm unfamiliar with children, as no doubt you observed. Take the horses into the stable yard — it's through that arch over there, I shall speak to Miss Sinclair and send word when I want Othello brought round to me.'

He had expected her to be waiting for him at the front door, but his arrival had gone unobserved and unannounced. Being obliged to hammer on the door was not something he was accustomed to, and not something he intended to make a habit of.

When a flustered servant girl eventually let him, in he was in a foul humour, and in two minds about whether to storm off in high dudgeon.

* * *

'Thank you so much, Lydia, for allowing me to read your novel. I was up all night finishing it. I've never read anything quite as good.'

'I have tried to combine the Gothic within a realistic setting. I am so pleased you enjoyed it, Viola — that has given me the impetus I need to take it to London.'

'Perhaps it might be wise to write an introductory letter to one or two companies rather than arrive with your manuscript under your arm.'

'I have decided not to do that, as that gives the publisher an opportunity to reject me without having seen my book. I believe I will get a better hearing if I appear in person.'

They were interrupted by an extremely upset maid. 'I beg your pardon, miss, but his grace is here and is in a frightful temper. He wanted to know why he had been ignored as he had been knocking at the front door for an age. He all but bit my head off when I said you were busy.'

Viola was on her feet in a trice. 'I shall go and find the children; I have left them on their own for far too long already.' She vanished in a flash of skirts, leaving Lydia to face the unwanted visitor alone.

'I hope you have shown his grace into the drawing room?'

'Yes, miss, and I asked him if he wanted any refreshments, and he told me to go away.'

'Please don't be upset, Mary, he's famous for his bad humour. I shall go and speak to him myself and see what has made him so cross.'

She was tempted to leave him kicking his heels for another ten minutes or so, but thought better of it. As he was already annoyed about being kept waiting, it would not be wise to exacerbate matters. If he had come over in his gig, she would have expected him to enter by the side door rather than come around to the front.

She pinned a pleasant smile on her face, checked that her skirts were hanging smoothly and there was no ink on her fingers, and then stepped into the drawing room. 'Good heavens! I did not expect to see you without your crutches so soon.' She had not intended to say this, but was so surprised to see him prowling about the drawing room with not even the slightest limp that she had been unable to keep the words back.

'My leg is mended, Miss Sinclair, and I rode over to see how you are all progressing with your riding. I did not expect to be left standing on your doorstep like an unwanted parcel.'

She couldn't stop an involuntary giggle at his analogy. The last thing she would have compared him to was a parcel. 'I can only apologise, your grace, but no one was aware you were here.'

'Do you find the situation amusing?'

She was about to apologise again, but then decided that in her own home she could do as she wished; if he didn't like the way she behaved, then he need not visit her here again.

'As a matter of fact, sir, I do. Describing yourself as a parcel appealed to my sense of the ridiculous. If you had said 'an unwanted panther' or 'mountain lion', I would have nodded and agreed with you.'

Then she saw the glimmer of amusement in his eyes and realised he had been teasing her, pretending to be angry at her amusement.

'Mountain lion? Panther? Are you saying that I resemble a feline?'

She gestured towards the seat before answering. He strolled across, flicked aside the tails of his jacket, and folded his long length onto the chair.

'You have a tendency to prowl, your grace, and the colouring of a panther.'

'I've been called worse in my time, my dear, and I'm not at all offended by your impertinence.'

She opened her mouth to protest, then saw he was laughing at her again. She rather liked this new version of the duke — she had not thought him a man with a sense of humour until now.

'I gather from your response to my maid that you have no wish for refreshments to be brought.'

A faint flush coloured his cheeks and he shrugged. 'I'm sorry if I upset your servant. I had no right to take it out on her.' He paused as if wondering whether he should continue, and she raised an eyebrow. He chuckled and resumed. 'I have never been obliged to knock on a front door myself before today — it is not something I wish to do again.'

Whatever she had expected him to say, it certainly was not this. She leaned forward in her chair, not sure if he was being serious or jesting again. 'If you don't knock on the door, how do you gain entry?'

'I expect the door to be opened before I arrive because a vigilant servant has seen me approaching. Failing that, a servant would do the knocking for me.'

She shook her head in disbelief. 'I had no idea that knocking on the door was so unacceptable amongst the toplofty members of society. Or is it just a duke who must not lower himself in this way?' She sat back in puzzlement. 'Last time you entered by the side door — that must have been a disagreeable experience for you, your grace.'

He nodded solemnly. 'It was indeed, my dear, and being obliged to go in by the back door is even worse than having to knock on the front.'

This badinage had gone on long enough. She wanted to know why he had come to see her. 'Your grace, forgive me, but was there something particular you wished to say to me that brought you here so unexpectedly?'

His eyes narrowed at her choice of words and she swallowed nervously. 'I came to enquire how the new governess is settling in, and if you are satisfied with her work.'

'That is doing it too brown, your grace, as we both know you have no interest whatsoever in Miss Carstairs. You must supply me with a better reason than that.'

This time his smile was genuine

— until that moment she had not understood just how attractive he was. Although there were deep lines etched on either side of his mouth from the years of pain he had endured, she now saw him as a handsome and charming man — not old at all.

'I am found out in my prevarication. I came, my dear, because I had nowhere else to go. I have not walked normally for five years. I just wished to share this good news with somebody.'

'And I'm glad that you chose to come here, your grace. I can imagine how wonderful it must be for you to be able to do the things that were impossible until now. By the way, thank you for your kind invitation to your party the day after tomorrow. Miss Carstairs and I are so looking forward to it.'

* * *

He had not known the governess was included. Digby had overstepped the mark there. He did not hide his expression of displeasure quickly enough, and the atmosphere in the room changed from relaxed to icy.

'I take it from your expression of disgust, your grace, that it was not you that invited us. We will not come: we have no wish to intrude at an event that is not meant for lesser mortals such as ourselves.'

She was on her feet and staring pointedly at the door, and he had no option but to do as she indicated. Now was not the time to explain his reaction had been because of the governess, that he truly wanted Miss Sinclair to be there. He was shocked that she considered herself on the same level as Miss Carstairs when she came from a good, if impoverished, family.

He rose smoothly and bowed formally. 'I bid you good afternoon, Miss Sinclair.'

She nodded, but did not curtsy. He strode out, wishing he had not been so maladroit — it was too long since he had spent time with a young lady of quality, and he was sadly out of practice.

When he stopped, he recalled that he had not sent word to the stables to ask for his horse to be brought round. His leg was aching like the very devil, and he feared he had overdone it today. To his surprise and delight, Bates was there and, without being asked, gave him a leg up into the saddle. For their return they took the short cut through the woods, and Everett was glad to be back. He was damned if he was going to limp his way into the house; he gritted his teeth and strode off as if there was nothing bothering him at all.

He now had to negotiate the enormous oak staircase that dominated the entrance hall, and he wasn't sure he could manage it without assistance. Then Bates was at his elbow, saying quietly, 'Lean on me, your grace, I'll get you to your apartment without mishap.'

Michaels took one look at him and tutted under his breath. 'I think you have been overdoing it, your grace, you won't want to be going down again today. I'll have your dinner brought up on a tray.'

Everett scarcely remembered being divested of his garments by both men. He raised and lowered his arms like a small child, and when his valet dropped a voluminous nightshirt over his head he did not protest.

He flopped back into bed with a sigh of relief. He closed his eyes and tried to encourage his knotted muscles to relax. The curtains on the enormous bed had been drawn around, giving him privacy and welcome darkness.

He dozed for a while, and when he awoke he was feeling much restored. He flinched when he moved his leg, but was grateful it did still respond to his command. He yelled for attention and Michaels appeared holding a tray.

'I have brought you a large whisky, your grace, and a jug of coffee.'

Everett pushed himself upright and shoved a few pillows behind him. 'Exactly what I would like, thank you.'

He was on his third cup when he heard a voice he recognised. Doctor Adams had been sent for. He was about to swing his legs to the floor when the young man came in and waved him back.

'Stay where you are, your grace, I think you have done more than enough walking today.'

'I overdid it. I was so pleased I could walk that I quite forgot the strictures you had given me. I sincerely hope I have not undone your excellent work by my foolishness.'

The physician examined his leg and got him to flex and bend it. 'No, your grace, everything is as it should be. The muscles on this leg are weak, and it will take some time for you to get the full strength back into them. You must take things easier in future — let nature take its course.'

'I give you my word I will rest tomorrow and the following day, and not do anything strenuous until the evening of the party.'

'I'm glad to hear it, sir. I shall leave you now. Do not get up again today.'

As soon as he was gone, Everett rang the bell that stood on the bedside table, and this time Bates appeared. 'Fetch me pen and paper, and something to lean on, I wish to write a letter. When I'm done, you can deliver it to the Dower House.'

10

When Lydia received the letter from the duke, she was tempted to tear it up without reading it, but thought better of it and broke the seal.

Miss Sinclair

I cannot remember ever having apologised for anything in my life before, and yet here I am tendering my apologies to you again. My only excuse for my appalling rudeness is that I have been brought up to think of myself as a superior being, and therefore have a tendency to consider everyone else as my inferior.

I would like to invite both you and Miss Carstairs to attend the party tomorrow. I will not take no for an answer. I shall send a carriage to collect you both at eight o'clock.

I am yours to command . . .

She wasn't sure if she was shocked or amused by his words. He had certainly apologised, he had issued a formal invitation to both her and her friend, but she was still unsure if he did consider them inferiors.

Fortunately, she had yet to tell Viola they had been uninvited, so she decided not to mention what had taken place that afternoon. The twins were in the garden with their nursemaid and she went to join them. Richard, Emma and their governess appeared shortly after this, and they played hide-and-seek until it was time for nursery tea.

She had asked for dinner to be served outside on the terrace. A trestle had been found in an outhouse and set up. Now, draped with a crisp white tablecloth and laid up with the best cutlery and crystalware, it looked quite magical.

Of course, they didn't change for dinner; there was no point in such an informal household. Viola joined her outside after she had supervised the older children's bedtime routine.

'I have not eaten *al fresco* for years,' the governess reflected happily. 'I think it an excellent notion. Being outside is a little more inconvenient for the staff, but I'm sure they won't mind. I know Cook much prefers to prepare a formal meal than send us up something on a tray each night.'

'I have asked Beth to put out anything she thinks will suit you — they are already arranged like an Indian bazaar over the furniture in my sitting room.'

'I do have suitable slippers and gloves — but I do not own a fan. Do you think I could borrow one of those?'

'Good heavens! I've never used one, and don't intend to start now. I'm hoping we can wander about outside as the invitation stated quite clearly it was an informal event. I'm glad there will be no dancing, as that is not one of my strengths.'

Viola laughed. 'I was obliged to instruct my previous charges in the art.

When we have dined, I shall teach you how to waltz and perform a country dance. I doubt, even if there is dancing at this event, there will be anything else you need to know.'

'But we have no music to accompany us.'

'I shall be the music as well as the instructor. You play the pianoforte beautifully, so you will have no difficulty learning these few basic steps.'

The air was filled with the enchanting song of the nightingales when they finally went inside. Although the candles had looked quite beautiful in the darkness, Lydia didn't like the way the moths were attracted to the flames, and was eager to go inside.

She had sent word upstairs so her maid was waiting for them. She beckoned her friend into her sitting room and gestured to the half-dozen gowns waiting to be inspected. Viola clapped her hands like a child and ran from one to the other, exclaiming in delight. Eventually, she settled on a cream silk with a pale green underskirt and matching flowers sewn around the neckline and hem.

'This is the most beautiful gown I have ever seen. Are you quite sure you wish to loan it to me?'

'It is not a loan, my dear, it is a gift. There are gloves and slippers to complete the ensemble — you must have those as well. I apologise for the lack of a fan, but I did not ask for any to be made up for me.'

They parted, both delighted with the result. Lydia had yet to decide which gown she was going to wear. She had asked her maid to put out all six new gowns she owned, as she thought Viola might not have been so ready to accept her gift if she believed these dresses were all she had.

Being in possession of five evening gowns was more than she had ever dreamed of, and far more than she would need. Even if in the future she was invited to something as prestigious as the event to be held tomorrow night, she saw no reason why she shouldn't wear the same ensemble again. As far as such people were concerned, she was a nonentity, not a person to take notice of, and therefore whatever she wore would be of no interest to those present.

Whilst busy folding up the gowns in preparation for placing them carefully on the shelves in her closet, Lydia made her selection. 'I think I will wear the emerald green,' she addressed her maid. 'I have my sister's emerald earbobs and necklace which will go perfectly with them. In fact, that was the reason I chose the material.'

'It's not the usual colour for an unmarried lady, miss, but with your dark colouring and green eyes, it will be perfect. You will be the belle of the ball.'

'It is not a ball, but an informal supper party. I have no wish to be the centre of attention, so perhaps I had better wear the pink damask instead.'

'Forgive me for saying so, miss, but I think that would be a mistake. You want to look your best, and this gown will make sure that you do.'

Reluctantly, Lydia agreed with her maid. Tomorrow might be the only opportunity she had to wear the emeralds. They had once belonged to a grandmother she had never met — they were the only things she owned of any value.

* * *

'Do you wish to inspect the arrangements, your grace?' Frobisher asked.

'No, I'm certain everything is exactly as it should be. I observed from my apartment several carriages turning into the drive. The first guests will be here in ten minutes.'

Everett had sent a carriage to collect the young ladies from the Dower House, and had been hoping they would be here first, but for some reason they had not as yet appeared. He had no intention of standing in the vast entrance hall bowing and smiling to everybody as they came in. His staff could greet his guests, and he would speak to them individually when they came into the drawing room, or joined him on the terrace.

The outside area looked magical tonight and would look even more so when it got dark. His gardeners had arranged flowers in every corner and entwined ivy in and out of the balustrade. The lanterns that hung in the trees were not yet alight as the sun was still shining.

He had expected a trio or a quartet at the most, but Digby had taken it upon himself to engage what looked like a small orchestra. From the screeching and wailing coming from the dozen or so musicians as they tuned up their instruments, he supposed they were about to start playing.

He had done as the doctor suggested and rested all day yesterday, and most of today, and now felt fitter than he had for years. His leg didn't ache, he was walking smoothly, and he had found himself agreeing there should be dancing after supper. He didn't intend to partake himself, but he would enjoy watching others prancing about the floor.

Even when he had been young and uninjured, he had never danced: it was not a pastime he found pleasurable. He much preferred to converse — or, even better, to play cards. Digby had assured him that at least half the gentleman would be happy to sit down with him to play Vingt-et-Un, Piquet or Loo.

There was a considerable advantage being a head taller than most of the gentlemen present, as it meant he could see who was moving in his direction and take appropriate action if he didn't wish to speak to them. The musicians were now playing, and the sweet sound echoed through the reception rooms: these had been cleared of all large furniture so there was room to move around freely. Small groups of chairs and tables had been positioned around the edge of the drawing room and ballroom. The second drawing room had been utilised as a card room, and the music room would be used for people to eat their supper.

The meal was to be served as a buffet, and his guests left to select what they wanted. There would be ample footmen around to serve beverages, and both tea and coffee available in the dining room later in the evening for those who wished for a non-alcoholic drink.

His eyes widened when he saw his physician talking to Miss Sinclair and the governess. He had only recognised her because of the startling colour of her companion's hair.

How could he have ever thought her plain? He was not the only gentleman glancing admiringly in her direction. The confection she was wearing was an unusual shade of green — emerald, he thought it might be called. Her hair was arranged in an elaborate style, and she was wearing what he was certain were expensive jewels around her neck and in her ears.

He was about to turn away from them when he overheard two matrons talking.

'My dear Lady Ponsonby, who is that young lady dressed so unsuitably? Such bright colours should only be worn by married women, not someone of her age and status.'

'And that other girl — such shockingly bright hair. I cannot abide red hair, and certainly not of such a shade as that. I much prefer a young lady with golden curls myself.'

He changed direction, and strode across to greet them as if they were close friends. 'Miss Sinclair, Miss Carstairs, thank you for gracing my humble abode this evening.'

They curtsied and he bowed. Miss Sinclair replied, smiling at him in a most particular way. 'Thank you for coming to greet us personally, your grace. I fear I have made the most dreadful blunder coming in this gown. I could not resist the colour as it matched my eyes.' She stopped and her cheeks flushed becomingly.

'I can assure you, your gown is perfect. You will, without doubt, be the most beautiful young lady present tonight.'

He offered her his arm, and was pleased to see that the doctor did the same for the governess. He guided her across the hall, the drawing room, and out onto the terrace.

'How beautiful you have made it look, your grace.' She glanced at him and he responded to her smile. 'Although I'm sure you actually had nothing at all to do with it yourself. Your staff have done an excellent job.'

'When the lanterns on the poles and in the trees are alight, it will look even more beautiful — Devil take it! Benji has followed you! I can see him hiding in the shrubbery over there.'

Instead of being shocked by his appalling language, she ran to the balustrade and followed his stare. 'Yes, I can see him. He is a very loyal and protective member of the family, and I must thank you again, your grace, for being so kind as to loan him to us.'

'He is yours to keep, my dear. I will have papers drawn up to that effect. He will never be happy anywhere but with you and the children.'

'Mr Digby told me he was your favourite hound. I wish there was a way we could all share him.'

*   *   *

Lydia was surprised at his reaction to her words. She had not said anything out of the ordinary. However, he looked at her strangely and then changed the subject.

'There will be dancing later, my dear. I hope you will stand up with me for at least one dance. I am sadly out of practice, but I'm sure you will not let me down.'

'I'm afraid I must decline your kind offer, your grace, as until last night I had no knowledge of any dance steps.

Miss Carstairs has done her best to instil the rudiments of a country dance and the waltz into my head, but I fear I should be a poor partner for you.'

His expression was as if she had been speaking to him in a foreign language. Then his mouth curved. 'Have I heard correctly, Miss Sinclair? You have just refused to dance with the most important person in the neighbourhood? Have you forgotten I am a duke, and an unmarried duke at that?'

She raised her hand to cover her mouth and try and push back the giggles that were fighting to escape. 'You're being ridiculous, but I must own that I much prefer you in this mode than when you are roaring and shouting at a person.'

'Either you will dance with me, my dear, or I shall not dance at all. Do you wish to be the young lady who ruined my evening?'

'We can hear the music perfectly well from the terrace, so I agree to dance one dance with you out here. However,

I refuse to expose my shortcomings in front of your neighbours. I've already garnered more than enough comments because of my gown.'

'Then it is agreed, we shall waltz out here. Forgive me, my dear, I must abandon you and talk to my other guests, or there will be wild speculation at my spending so much time in your company.' His smile made her toes curl in her slippers and her bodice feel uncomfortably tight. He really was a most attractive gentleman when he put his mind to it.

She had no idea why he had paid her so much attention this evening, or why he wished to dance with her. Up until this point in their brief acquaintance, they had been mostly at daggers drawn, or cordially disliked each other.

Perhaps she had been misjudging him, and his curmudgeonly behaviour had been a direct result of being incapacitated; a fine, athletic gentleman such as himself would obviously resent being obliged to be pushed around in a wheeled chair.

There was no sign of her friend or the young man who had been introduced to them as Dr Adams. Lydia had no intention of remaining on the terrace alone, so decided to wander around the garden and avoid the press of people in the drawing room.

The grass was still dry, the evening dew not yet damp underfoot. With luck, she would be able to make her way to the maze without spoiling either her slippers or her gown. Only as she was halfway to her destination did she think about how conspicuous she might be if anyone happened to look out of the drawing room windows, or wander onto the terrace.

Then a wet nose was pressed into her hand. 'Benji, how good it is to see you here tonight. I'm going to walk around the maze, and will be glad of your company, as I doubt that you will get lost even if I do.'

The fact that the animal would leave

hairs on her skirts did not bother her. The clipped hedges were shoulder height, and she certainly wouldn't be able to scramble over the top in order to make her way out.

'Well, Benji, now that we are here I think we must investigate, don't you?'

She noticed there was a terracotta pot standing at the entrance in which there were half a dozen small flags. Presumably one took one of these so that it could be waved in order to attract attention if one became disorientated.

The grass inside was neatly clipped and dry underfoot. The paths were wide enough to allow her to pass through without danger of miring her gown. With a flag in one hand and the dog at her other side, she ventured inside.

The dog moved in front, and she followed him as he appeared to know where he was going. After a few minutes they arrived at the centre, where there was a marble bench upon which a visitor might rest before attempting the return journey.

From this vantage point, she could see the house in all its splendour. All the downstairs windows were ablaze with candlelight, and the sound of music and merriment drifted across the grass. There were several couples on the terrace, but none of them were looking in her direction, and for that she was grateful.

'Come along, you must lead me out, as . . . ' Before she could complete her sentence to the dog, his head came up, his ears twitched, and he vanished down one of the pathways, leaving her on her own.

Despite calling him several times, she got no response, and a few minutes later she saw him tearing across the open grass after an unfortunate rabbit.

She had paid no attention to the turns she had taken in order to reach the centre of the maze, and now must try and find her way back without the assistance of her erstwhile companion.

11

'Miss Carstairs, I am in search of Miss Sinclair as she has promised to stand up with me for the first waltz. Do you have any idea where she might be?'

'No, your grace, I have not seen her for this age. Last time I was with her she was on the terrace, and that was over an hour ago.'

Everett nodded and strode outside, determined to find his reluctant partner. A flash of green caught his eye. Good God! The ridiculous girl had got herself lost in the maze. What had possessed her to venture in there at this time of night?

Regardless of what any spectators might think of his behaviour, he broke into a run. This was the first time he had attempted to move at more than at a sober walk, and he hoped his newly-set leg would survive the experience. He was not stupid enough to go full-pelt, but kept to a steady jog.

When he was close enough to be heard without raising his voice, he called out, 'Miss Sinclair, if you remain stationary I shall come and find you.'

'I'm so glad you have come, your grace, I have been wandering about in here like a lost sheep forever. Benji led me in, but then abandoned me in preference to chasing a rabbit. I've whistled and called but he has not returned to guide me out again.'

He had spent many happy hours in the maze, so knew every twist and turn, and reached her in moments. She looked rather dishevelled: the hem of her gown was damp from the evening dew and her slippers were equally mired.

'I'm still at a loss to know why you decided to come here in the first place.'

'I know it was foolish of me, but I do not like crowds, particularly of people I do not know. I only intended to be gone for half an hour at the most. I take it you came in search of me because it is time for our dance.'

He led her back into the centre of the maze where there was room to move. 'Stand still: I will attempt to remove the debris from your person and make you presentable again. It is fortunate that your hair has remained in place, as I doubt I could remedy that. My experience as a lady's maid is somewhat limited.'

She laughed at his remark. 'I should hope so, your grace. Is my gown quite ruined by this nonsense?'

'No, you are beautiful still.' He offered his arm and she slipped hers through it. He was beginning to enjoy being her escort.

When they were halfway across the grass, the missing dog bounded up to them, something gripped in his jaws that he guessed was a dead rabbit. 'No, Benji, take it away.'

The animal stopped, cocked his head, and waited for his companion to confirm the order.

'Horrible dog, I've no wish to receive that present! Take it home and give it to someone in the kitchen.'

Benji wagged his tail and ran off into the darkness as if he had understood every word spoken.

'It has taken him more than an hour to find that wretched rabbit. I thought hounds were hunters. Benji is obviously not particularly good at this pastime.'

'You should be pleased, my dear — that is the first rabbit he has caught. I'm sure you will receive a steady supply now he has got the hang of it.'

They fell silent for a while as they approached the house. He wished to dance with her, to hold her in his arms and whirl her around the floor.

In the deserted entrance hall, she hesitated. 'Forgive me, your grace, will you excuse me from dancing tonight? My slippers are saturated and I did not bring a spare pair. I cannot venture anywhere that I will be seen with wet shoes.'

'You can hardly remain out here on your own; that will be considered even more peculiar than wearing such a gown.'

Her fingers tightened on his arms. 'I thought you told me I looked stunning, your grace. Now the true story is emerging.'

For a horrible moment, he thought she was speaking seriously, but then she laughed softly.

'You are fishing for compliments, my dear. I told you how lovely you look, and I stand by that opinion. However, as you so rightly pointed out earlier, there are several less broad-minded matrons who disagree with my opinion. It is better not to upset them further.'

'Then I shall have to ask for the carriage to return me home. I shall be sorry to leave, for I was rather looking forward to my supper. Mr Digby tells me you have a French chef employed here.'

'You will not go home. That is not what I meant at all. Do you play cards?'

She looked somewhat surprised by his abrupt question, but rallied. 'I do indeed, sir, but do not gamble.'

'Then we shall be partners in a game or two of Whist. Your slippers will soon dry, and will not be visible when you are sitting at a card table. I can assure you that nobody will be aware of your wild behaviour.'

'Wild? That is hardly a polite comment, your grace.' She laughed, and came with him willingly to the card room. Then she squeezed his arm. 'Forgive me for asking, but is your leg troubling you?'

He was about to deny this, but something made him speak the truth. 'I have rather overexerted myself this evening. Thank you for your concern, my dear, it is much appreciated. Is that why you refused to dance?'

'It is. I don't give a fig for what others say of me. If I had thought you able, I should have insisted on dancing. No, do not poker up at me, you must not take offence because I have mentioned your infirmity. Good heavens, a few weeks ago you were unable to get about at all, and look at you now!'

He smiled ruefully. 'Look at me indeed, my dear. A sorry specimen who cannot fulfil his promise to dance with his partner.'

'You are not a sorry anything. You are a handsome gentleman in his prime, and no doubt the most eligible *parti* in the kingdom.' Her smile made something strange happen to his stomach. 'Fear not, I have no designs on you. In fact, you are safer with me than with any other young lady present. I have no intention of marrying, however eligible the gentleman might be — do you wish me to tell you my darkest secret?'

He was so stunned by her compliment he could not form a coherent answer, and merely nodded.

'I am a writer. I have just completed my first novel.'

★ ★ ★

If she had announced she was a devil worshipper, he could not have looked more horrified. 'Do you have an aversion to novelists, your grace? I can assure you that apart from having a prodigious amount of ink upon my fingers most of the time, I'm perfectly normal.'

'I have heard young ladies speak of wishing to write a book, but one who has actually done this is something else again.' The tension in his arm relaxed, and he nodded and smiled benevolently. 'If scribbling away in secret is what makes you happy, my dear, then who am I to cavil? It's not as though you intend to have your work seen by the general public.'

She was about to contradict his statement, but thought better of it. It was none of his business if she had her book published or not — but it might be wiser to use a *nom de plume* and not her own name in order to avoid unnecessary confrontation.

'I'm sure you would consider it

romantic nonsense, your grace, far below your notice. I do not enjoy painting watercolours or embroidery, so write instead. Of course, I have my music as well to occupy my time, when I am not running the house or organising the lives of the four children in my care.'

'How old are you?'

This abrupt question took her aback; she was tempted to give him a fallacious reply. 'I will be three and twenty on my next name day in May. Why do you ask? I thought it was considered indelicate to ask a lady's age. How old are you?' She made her question as abrupt as his and waited for him to scowl at her.

Instead, he chuckled. 'Hoist by my own petard, my dear. I shall be three and thirty my next name day; it too is in May. I know you say you have no wish to be married, but you are too young to be kept cloistered in the country with only a governess for company.'

'Viola is as well-bred as I am. She has to work for her living because her mama died, her father remarried, and her stepmother told her to leave. I consider her a dear friend, and not just an employee.'

'I apologise if I have caused offence. I'm not criticising. Indeed, my physician appears to be quite taken with her, so maybe you will not have her in your employ for as long as you hope.' He picked up a pack of cards and raised an eyebrow.

'Now, are we to play cards or not? There has been more than enough chit-chat for one night, in my opinion.'

They played for an hour, and honours were even at the end of it. 'My slippers are quite dry, so it will be safe for me to venture from here.'

'Excellent. They are to play a waltz as the supper dance, and I intend that you shall stand up with me for that.'

He appeared to have quite forgotten her saying she would only dance on the terrace and not in public, and it was too late to argue. He whisked her from the card room, across the spacious entrance hall, and into the ballroom before she had time to draw breath.

As they arrived, the musicians played the opening chords of the dance. The other couples stepped aside to allow him to lead her out, and she wished the boards would open up and swallow her.

'This is intolerable, your grace. I shall make a sad mull of it, and both your reputation and mine will be in tatters.'

'Follow my lead, my dear, and you shall not go wrong. Surely you are aware that someone as important as myself can do no wrong?'

Despite her reservations, after the first few bars she began to enjoy the experience of being held in a gentleman's arms — especially one as tall and commanding as the duke. She could hardly credit that a few days ago he had been hopping around on crutches, for he was as graceful and sure-footed as any other gentleman present.

He guided her around the floor with

expertise and she relaxed into his embrace. 'I thought you said that you were an indifferent dancer, your grace; that is a Banbury tale, and well you know it.'

'I always considered myself a poor dancer, but then I had not danced with you until tonight.' She was disappointed when the final chords were played and the couples bowed and curtsied to each other. He had his arm loosely around her waist, and his fingertips brushing against her made her feel flustered and overheated.

He nodded towards a small table in the music room set out for supper — it was laid for two. 'See, we shall not have to scramble for our food as lesser mortals do.'

She was uncertain how to respond to this remark, so ignored it. She had become increasingly aware that there were several tabbies scowling at her for monopolising the duke. This would not do.

'Thank you for dancing with me, but

I think you would be advised to sit elsewhere for supper, as you have already spent far too much time with me.'

She slipped her arm from his, smiled politely and almost ran to the stairs. The ladies' restroom was up there; she could spend half an hour or more repairing her appearance without garnering too much comment. Hopefully, when she returned to the fray she could find herself a less conspicuous place to sit.

As she reached the hall, there was a hideous howling coming from the park, which made her stop. Benji was making it very plain he wished her to come out and join him. She needed no further excuse to return home. She wouldn't bother to call for the carriage, but walk the mile with the dog as company.

There was more than enough light from the full moon to make this easy. She returned to the restroom and found her slipper bag. It was the work of moments to exchange her dancing slippers for the sturdier versions she had travelled in.

★ ★ ★

Benji joined her when she was fifty yards from the house and frolicked around her, eager to demonstrate his pleasure at her appearance.

'Be still, you silly dog, you have caused more than enough upset for one night.'

An evening gown was not well-suited to a walk through the woods, as the flimsy material was likely to get snagged on the brambles and branches. Therefore, she decided to take the track that vehicles used. The weather was warm and the moonlight sufficient for her to see; the only risk she was taking was that of spoiling the hem of her gown.

The hound trotted along beside her, and obviously had no intention of dashing off to investigate the interesting noises that came from the shrubbery on either side the path. She was holding the skirt of her gown in either hand in the vain hope that it would suffer no damage from her evening stroll.

The sound of the orchestra travelled through the night, and was a welcome accompaniment to her walk. Then she realised that, in her eagerness to leave, she had forgotten to send a message to Viola. Her friend would no doubt be looking for her — and, when she was not to be found anywhere on the premises, might well set up a search party.

If this was done, then inevitably the duke would wish to be part of that group. Lydia was concerned he had already overused his recently repaired leg, and she had no wish for him to do himself permanent harm on her behalf.

With a sigh of exasperation, she spoke out loud to the dog. 'Benji, I fear I must go back and find someone to take a message to Viola. It is most vexatious, but I have no option. Are you going to accompany me?'

The dog sat down in the middle of

the track, his long tail swishing the dirt from side to side. He showed no inclination to come with her, and she supposed he intended to wait where he was for her return.

She was certain she had not been gone more than twenty minutes, and with luck could get word to her friend before she became anxious. Unfortunately, she met no lurking footman on her return journey, which meant she would be obliged to make her way around to the terrace. She had no intention of entering the main reception rooms as her appearance would no longer pass muster. She had caused more than enough excitement tonight just by wearing a gown of emerald green when all the other unmarried young ladies wore pastel shades or white.

'Where the devil have you been?' the duke barked from just above her, and she was so startled she put her foot through her gown and fell in an undignified heap to the ground. She wasn't sure if she was more upset by his appalling language or by the fact that she had twisted her ankle.

Then he was beside her. 'I beg your pardon, sweetheart, I should not have yelled like that. Take my hand, and let me help you up.'

'I fear I have twisted my ankle, your grace, and cannot easily stand.'

'Put your arm around my neck and I will carry you.'

'I'll do no such thing; I'm perfectly capable of making my way to my carriage if you would be so good as to lend me your arm.'

He offered his hand and she took it, but couldn't restrain a yelp of pain as she straightened up. Before either of them could react, Benji appeared and hurled himself at the duke, growling ferociously, sending them both to the ground again.

She was terrified the animal would savage him, believing he was the cause of her distress. She need not have worried on the duke's behalf.

'Get off, you stupid animal! You are making matters worse.'

The growling stopped and the dog sat down with them on the grass, presumably thinking this was a fine game that he would play too.

'We cannot remain here indefinitely, but I fear we are going to need assistance if we are both to regain our feet without further injury.'

'I believe I can hear someone on the terrace. I shall call out — I know your voice is far louder, your grace, but it will be less shocking if I do so.' She was trying to keep the mood light, to not dwell on why he could not get himself to his feet without aid. She had landed painfully on her injured ankle, and was certain she would not be able to walk at all even with an arm to lean on.

To her relief, he laughed. 'Whoever is up there, we are in need of your help.' His voice carried wonderfully well, and would no doubt be heard by everyone in the ballroom.

It was Viola who replied. 'I have been

looking for you this age, Lydia! Doctor Adams is with me and we are coming at once to your side.'

The duke explained how they came to be in this predicament, and she was delighted to see him able to stand upright once he had been hauled to his feet.

'Miss Sinclair, let me examine your ankle before I attempt to move you,' the doctor said.

'I should much prefer to go home and have my ankle seen to there. I have sprained it before now, a cold compress is all I require. There's no need . . . '

'I'll brook no argument, young lady; you will allow my physician to attend to you, there's a good girl.' The duke turned to Viola. 'Miss Carstairs, if you would be so kind as to find a servant and have them bring around your carriage? The doctor can carry Miss Sinclair to it once he has established there's no serious damage.'

When the doctor had concluded his examination, he sat back. 'You are right, nothing broken. However, it is a bad sprain, and you will need to keep it elevated for several days.'

'Thank you, I will certainly do that.'

He picked her up with no difficulty and carried her around to the turning circle, where by some miracle the carriage was already waiting.

12

'There's no need for you to return with me, Viola, I have no wish to spoil your evening too.'

'Good heavens, Lydia, I've no intention of remaining here without you.' Miss Carstairs stepped nimbly into the carriage, and a waiting footman put up the steps and closed the door.

Everett would have liked to go with them, but thought better of it. No doubt there would already be gossip and speculation about his interest in Miss Sinclair, and he had no wish to add fuel to the fire.

He turned abruptly to the doctor who was standing beside him. 'Go on, man, don't stand there gawping. You must go with Miss Sinclair and attend to her ankle. The carriage will bring you back when you are done.'

The doctor decided not to argue

— which was wise — but as the vehicle was already in motion, he had no option but to swing onto the back step and cling on like a servant. Then Everett noticed Benji had joined the cavalcade and was trotting along beside the carriage. He couldn't prevent his chuckle.

He had always considered himself a sensible and staid individual, but tonight he had behaved quite out of character. God knew what the doctor thought of him — but he cared little for that as long as Miss Sinclair was taken care of.

His inclination was to retreat to his study and let the party continue without him, but this would cause even more comment. His leg ached like the very devil and he would make this an excuse to sit somewhere quietly for the remainder of the evening.

Eventually the final tune was played, the last hand of cards completed, and his guests were ready to depart. He was congratulated on a splendid evening, and cordially invited to visit with his neighbours whenever he was in the vicinity.

He left his staff to put matters right downstairs, and made his slow and painful way to his apartment. Tonight, he was glad of his valet's attentions, as he doubted he could have disrobed himself.

'You look done in, your grace, forgive me for saying so. You need to rest tomorrow.'

'I certainly do. Please don't disturb me in the morning. I shall ring when I need you.'

The house settled into silence, and Everett tried to relax. However, his mind was racing and full of thoughts, most of them involving the infuriating but delectable Miss Sinclair.

He had intended to find her a suitable husband, but this no longer appealed to him as a solution. The thought of her in bed with another man made his stomach lurch unpleasantly. She had no wish to marry, and he would not encourage her to do so — he would be content to have her living with the children and the governess in the Dower House, as long as there were no gentleman callers.

He flexed his injured leg, and was pleased when it responded without too much pain. He would ride over tomorrow and see how the patient did; it would be uncivil not to do so. As he was drifting off to sleep, something most disturbing occurred to him.

As far as he was aware, Adams had not returned with the carriage — and this could mean the injury was far worse than first thought, and he had remained at the patient's side to minister to her. Everett was now wide awake again. He would not be able to settle until he discovered for himself that all was well.

He reached out his hand to ring for his valet, and then decided it would be unfair to rouse the man from his slumbers. His leg no longer hurt as much as it had before; he would find something to wear, and ride over to see nothing untoward had taken place.

He was dressed and on his way downstairs, candlestick held aloft, less than two hours since he had retired. To his astonishment, the chaos he had left downstairs was no more, and the house had been returned to its normal pristine cleanliness.

The side door was the easiest to unbolt, and he had no need to use the candle once he was outside. The moon was bright, the evening warm; he could manage without additional illumination.

Unlike many of his peers, he preferred his horses to live outside as nature intended during the summer months. The grooms brought in those that would be needed at dawn each day. This meant there would be an empty stable yard and he must catch himself a mount from the home paddock.

He snatched up a bridle, made his way quietly to the fence, and whistled. Immediately there was movement, and the sound of a horse cantering towards him. His stallion always came when he called.

'Othello, we are going on an adventure together. Hold still whilst I put on your bridle, and then I shall use the fence as a mounting block.'

The horse was unbothered by his unusual behaviour. Everett prayed he would still be able to ride bareback after so long. The last thing he needed was to take a tumble.

He untied the gate and led the horse through before swinging onto its back. It had been years since he had ridden without a saddle, but one didn't forget this sort of skill. He clicked his tongue, his mount moved away smoothly, and soon they were cantering along the path that led to the Dower House.

* * *

Richard was woken up by Benji scratching at the bedroom door. He crept out of bed and slipped into his sister's room in order to wake her but not the twins, who were sleeping soundly in the big bed. 'Benji wants us. Are you coming?'

He didn't bother to find his slippers, and neither did she — together, in their nightclothes, they crept to the door and slowly opened it expecting the dog to rush in and flatten them as he frequently did. Instead, he was standing in the passageway, wagging his tail and glancing anxiously down the stairs.

'He wants us to go with him — I hope there isn't a burglar,' Emma said.

'Do we need to get a candle?' Richard wasn't sure there was sufficient light coming in through the window at the end of the passage to descend the stairs safely.

'There isn't time; I can hear somebody outside.'

The dog was standing by the front door, whining softly. Richard ran to the door and spoke to whoever was behind it.

'I can't open this door as I don't have

the key. If you care to come to the side, I will let you in.'

There was a muffled reply and the sound of a man's steps retreating to the side of the house.

His sister grabbed his arm and pinched it painfully. 'You shouldn't have done that,' she whispered. 'We don't know who it is. It might be someone come to murder us in our beds.'

He shrugged his arm away. 'Don't be silly, Benji knows who it is.'

Only as he was sliding the bolt back did it occur to him the person on the other side of the door might be known to the dog, but not to them. He also belatedly considered the fact that no sensible person arrived at a house uninvited in the middle of the night.

The door swung open, and to his horror the duke stepped in. He wasn't sure he liked this gentleman very much — he was too tall, too dark, and too fierce.

'Good heavens! What are you two

doing down here in your nightclothes?'
He leaned down to pat the dog, who
seemed delighted to see their unexpected guest.

'Aunt Lydia is in bed, your grace,
and so is everybody else. Benji fetched
us to open the door for you. Is there
something wrong? Is that why you are
here when everyone is asleep?'

'Shall we go somewhere more comfortable to talk, children? What about
the kitchen? I expect it's warm in there,
and we can find ourselves something
tasty to eat and drink.'

This seemed like a good idea, and
Richard thought that perhaps he wasn't
such a bad fellow after all. 'Cook and
the other maids sleep upstairs, so they
won't hear us. I know where there's a
plum cake, and there's always fresh
milk in the pantry on the slate shelf.'

He dashed off with the dog beside
him and led the duke into the kitchen.
In here the floor was stone, and his bare
feet were becoming numb from the
cold.

To his astonishment, the duke picked him up and sat him on the long table that filled the centre of the room. 'Here, young man, you will be warmer with your feet off the flags.'

His sister didn't wait to be plucked from the floor, but scrambled up herself; and they sat side by side, their bare legs swinging, watching open-mouthed as his grace set about making them a midnight feast.

'I think hot milk with cinnamon and sugar is called for — does that seem acceptable to you?'

There were now half a dozen candles burning merrily as his grace had used the embers in the stove to light them.

'That sounds lovely, your grace — are you sure you can manage on your own?' Emma asked, more out of politeness than a desire to actually get down herself and assist him.

'I'm perfectly capable of heating up some milk, sweetheart, but I might need further directions to discover the aforementioned cake.'

Within a short space of time, the feast was ready, and Richard finally felt emboldened to ask the question that was hanging in the air between them. They had talked about the dog, the ponies, and the weather, but so far they had all avoided the reason why they were all sitting in the kitchen.

'I expect you were fast asleep when your aunt came home. She took a tumble and twisted her ankle, and the doctor travelled here with her in the carriage to attend to it. As he failed to return and tell me what happened, I came to see for myself that nothing untoward had taken place.'

'We didn't know Aunt Lydia had hurt herself. In fact, we didn't know anything about it at all.' He was beginning to warm to his theme. 'In fact, your grace, I don't even know if she is actually here. Do you think she could be lying dead in a ditch somewhere?'

He didn't wait for an answer, but jumped down from his perch on the table and ran to the door. 'I shall go up and investigate. I think you had better stay here, as I don't think Aunt Lydia would like to see you prowling about without her knowledge.'

He left his sister to entertain their guest and scampered upstairs, his feet silent on the boards. He hesitated outside her bedroom door, wondering if he should knock, or just peep in to see if she was there.

After a few moments, he decided he would try and see if she was indeed within. With luck, he could do this without waking her up and having to give a long explanation as to why he was there. For some reason, he was quite sure she would insist, damaged ankle or not, on coming down and speaking her mind to the duke.

Slowly he turned the knob and put his ear to the space. He could hear nothing, so pushed it open a little further. Silence. He slipped in and stood for a moment trying to recall exactly where the large bed was situated in the darkness.

All might have been well if Benji hadn't decided to join in with this game of hide-and-seek and bounded through the door. Richard flung himself on the dog in a vain attempt to stop him, and was dragged, feet flailing, across the room. On the way, he knocked over two side tables, and a candlestick landed painfully on his head. The resulting noise was enough to wake the dead.

★ ★ ★

Lydia sat up in bed as if stuck by a hatpin. 'Good Lord, what on earth are you doing in here, Richard?'

'I was trying to stop Benji from jumping on you, Aunt Lydia. I'm sorry if I woke you up.'

'I should think you have woken up the entire household.' Sitting up so suddenly had jarred her sprained ankle, and she was loath to get out of bed, but felt she probably had to in order to investigate.

241

Then Viola rushed in. 'I heard the most dreadful noise, whatever is going on in here? What are you doing out of bed, young man?'

As her friend had brought with her a lit candle, Lydia was now able to see that there was no real harm done. 'Richard, please pick up the tables and the candlestick.' She snapped her fingers at Benji then pointed to the door, and the dog slunk out, knowing he had transgressed.

'I am waiting, Richard, for you to tell me why you are running about the place in the middle of the night in your nightshirt.'

Her nephew looked from his governess to her and bit his lip. There was more to this than a childish prank.

'I shall tell you, but you won't be pleased. His grace came to visit, and Emma and I had to go down to let him in. We were having . . . '

'The duke is here? Whatever madness made him come like this?'

Richard moved closer and smiled.

'He thought you might not have got home safely, and wished to check for himself. I was going to tell you that he is making us hot milk with cinnamon, and Emma is finding us a slice of cake. May I be excused to go down and eat it?'

Lydia's head was spinning and she could scarcely form a coherent thought. She waited for Viola to intervene, take charge of the situation, but nothing came from that quarter. This was something she had to deal with herself.

'You must give his grace a message from me. Would you please tell him that I should be delighted to see him tomorrow afternoon, when the house is awake and I downstairs to receive him? Can you remember all that?'

He nodded. 'And the midnight feast?'

'Very well, you may have your milk and cake, but then you and Emma must escort the duke from the house and lock the door behind him. You will not be above a quarter of an hour. I shall leave my bedchamber door open so that you may say good night to me when you return to bed.'

He dashed off, leaving her alone with Viola. 'It is quite beyond my comprehension why a rational gentleman such as his grace should think it acceptable to visit here like this.'

'According to Richard, my dear, he was anxious for your safety. However, it is quite extraordinary, I agree. No doubt all will be explained to you when he makes a formal call tomorrow afternoon. Do you wish me to remain with you until the children come up, so I can see them safely to their beds?'

'No, there's no need for you to be awake as well. If it wasn't for my wretched ankle, I should go down and throw him out myself. Imagine his reaction if *I* had turned up on *his* doorstep like this!'

Her friend laughed. 'I think that he would have whisked you inside to his bedroom before you could say anything at all. There would be only one reason a lady would make a midnight visit to a gentleman.'

Lydia caught her breath and her skin prickled unpleasantly. She was glad the room was so dim and her friend couldn't see her painful blushes. 'Oh, my word! Surely he wasn't coming here to . . . to . . . ' She could not complete the sentence.

'Of course not, I was jesting. Although I must own I am curious as to his reasons for coming. I am certain he does not intend to make you his mistress, so the only other explanation is that he wishes to make you his wife.'

'That is the most ridiculous thing I've ever heard. He could marry any young lady in the kingdom — why should he settle his interest on me?'

'I've no idea — it doesn't make any sense, does it? I bid you good night, again, and will see you in the morning to continue this interesting conversation.'

Whilst Lydia waited for the children to come back, she had ample time to dwell on what had transpired. The more she thought about it the more flustered and uncomfortable she became.

Her niece and nephew appeared in less than the allotted time, apologised again, and skipped off to bed. A few moments later, she was certain she heard the sound of a horse cantering up the path that led through the woods to the big house.

13

Everett stood in the darkness outside the side door, having been all but ejected from the premises by two children. He smiled ruefully at his predicament. It served him right for behaving like the veriest nincompoop. What in God's name had possessed him to rush over here in this manner?

His horse was contentedly grazing, and whickered a soft greeting when he whistled. He twisted the mane around his hand and then, somewhat awkwardly, vaulted onto the stallion's back.

'Home, old fellow, I need my sleep.'

He dismounted by the gate into the meadow, unlatched it, removed the bridle, and his mount trotted obediently inside to join his fellow equines. Othello got on well with the geldings, but his head groom was careful to keep the mares in a paddock on the other side of the stables.

Once in the safety of his own apartment, he tossed his clothes in a heap on the floor and tumbled into bed. This time, he was so fatigued he was asleep immediately, and didn't wake until Michaels drew back the shutters.

'Good morning, your grace; you asked me not to disturb you, but Mr Digby wishes to speak to you most urgently.'

'What time is it?'

'A little after ten o'clock, sir.'

Everett rubbed his eyes and yawned loudly. He then saw his discarded garments on the floor and recalled his exploits. He could think of only one reason that Digby wanted to see him immediately. Someone had seen him riding to the Dower House and drawn their own conclusions.

'Send word for breakfast to be served, and tell Digby to join me in the breakfast room.'

He was halfway through shaving

when something occurred to him. He couldn't stop his mouth from curving. He had jumped out of bed and come into his dressing room, and not for one moment thought about his damaged leg. It didn't ache, it worked as well as it had used to — there was no doubt about it, Dr Adams was an outstanding surgeon.

He shrugged into his clean shirt, tucked the tails neatly between his legs, and was halfway into his breeches when his valet returned.

'Which coat do you wish to wear this morning, your grace?'

'Whatever comes to hand first, I'm in a hurry. Just make sure my waistcoat complements my outfit.' In less than half an hour, he was striding through the house on his way to speak to his man of affairs.

Digby was pacing the chamber, his expression anxious. 'I'm sorry to disturb you, your grace, but this matter could not wait.'

'I must eat; you must explain your

concerns whilst I do so.' The duke strode to the side table and picked up a plate. 'I hope you will join me?'

'Your grace, I cannot eat until I have told you why I've come.'

Everett put down his plate and faced the man. 'Well, out with it — it must be something serious to have you looking so pale.'

'I have just had word from a firm of lawyers who represent the interests of one Mr Castleford. It would seem you are not the children's guardian after all. There is an uncle, and he is on his way here to demand that you hand the children over.'

'Why is that a disaster? I have become fond of them, but they will do better with a close relative.'

'Miss Sinclair, your grace . . . are you as sanguine about her leaving?'

He was about to say that he was, but the words stuck behind his teeth. It was as if a curtain had been lifted and he could suddenly see clearly into the chamber beyond. His desire to get on his feet so quickly, his insistence of there being a grand party, the ponies and the little mare — and then his ridiculous performance last night — all these now made perfect sense.

He tottered to a chair and collapsed upon it. He closed his eyes to try and order his chaotic thoughts. 'You have seen what I did not until this moment, my friend. I am in love with her — I should be bereft without her in my life.'

Everett glanced up, expecting to see Digby looking suitably sombre at this news. After all, Miss Sinclair — no, she would be Lydia to him in future — was hardly the sort of young lady a man in his position should be marrying.

Instead, his companion was beaming. 'Excellent, excellent, your grace. In which case, there is no problem — the children go, but Miss Sinclair will stay as your wife.'

There was something not quite right about this suggestion. 'No, the children must stay with me. Lydia would be devastated to lose those she has nurtured from their infancy.'

He slammed his fist down on the table, making the cutlery jump and Digby step back in shock. 'Come, tell me; what must we do to make sure this uncle does not take them away from us?'

'I will investigate the matter further, your grace, now I know your preferences. I shall set matters in hand to make this arrangement legal. This house will come alive again with four children running about in it, and no doubt you will add to the nursery in due course yourselves.'

Digby looked hopefully at the laden buffet.

'Then be seated, old friend, for I shall serve you today. You have looked after my interests and put up with my rudeness these past five years, and I could not have survived without you.'

'If you are sure, your grace, then I should be delighted to join you to break my fast. So much excitement is not good for a man of my age. You know, perhaps it is time for you to find someone younger . . . '

'I'll be damned if I will; you are as much part of this family as the children and Miss Sinclair. I shall put a little of everything on your plate and do the same for myself. Help yourself to coffee, small beer, or whatever you fancy from the table.'

He piled his plate equally high and tucked in with relish. He had things to do, and would need all his strength if he was to convince his beloved that she should give up her freedom and become his duchess. She was not like other young ladies: she would not accept his proposal unless she was in love with him and could not live without him at her side.

When he was replete, he dropped his cutlery noisily on the empty plate. 'Get your secretary to have the nursery floor redecorated, I want everything perfect when they move in here.'

'I shall do that at once, your grace. Perhaps it might be sensible to employ more indoor staff?'

'I shall leave that to you, Digby, as I always do. I have to speak to Lydia at once.'

★　★　★

Lydia found it impossible to slumber, and as dawn lightened the room sufficiently for her to move around safely, she swung her feet to the floor. If she hopped, and used chairs and tables to lean on, she was sure she could find herself something to wear and get dressed.

It took her longer than she'd expected, but after half an hour she was satisfied with her appearance. She pinned her plait around her head in a coronet, and was then ready to descend.

Doctor Adams had been quite clear that she was to remain upstairs with her foot elevated for at least two days — but fiddlesticks to that! She could not remain incarcerated in her apartment a moment longer. She needed to be outside in the fresh air, regardless of her injury.

Her ankle no longer ached, and only hurt when her she put her weight on it. She hopped as quietly as she could to the stairs, and then slowly lowered herself until she was sitting on the top step. Going down on her derrière was undignified, but perfectly efficient.

Early morning light was filtering in through the windows throughout the house, making it easy for her to get about without the danger of falling, or the necessity to carry a candlestick. Then she saw exactly the items she needed — she had quite forgotten there was a wooden box in one corner of the hall containing a variety of walking sticks and canes. She selected two, and used them in the same way that she had seen his grace using his crutches.

It took a few attempts, but her ploy worked wonderfully. Now she was able to get about without putting her damaged ankle to the ground.

The side door was easy to unbolt

— which, no doubt, was why the children had let his grace in that way. As soon as she was in the garden, hearing the swelling sound of the dawn chorus that filled the air, she felt immeasurably better.

There was a convenient bench placed in a honeysuckle arbour not far from the side door, and this would be ideal for her to use whilst she gathered her thoughts.

The duke would be coming to see her, and she needed to have things straight in her mind before he arrived. She had told him to come in the afternoon, but doubted he would stick to that suggestion. He would arrive whenever he felt like it — probably immediately after breakfast.

When she had first met him, she had disliked him. Although they had only been in each other's company a few hours since then, she had begun to change her mind. But liking somebody was not the same as wishing to become their wife.

She snorted inelegantly at this ridiculous notion. Just because he had behaved out of character didn't mean he was intending to make her an offer.

What would she do if he did? Would being married to him be so very awful? The children would remain in her care until they were grown, and she would no longer have sole responsibility for their upbringing. That could only be a good thing, as it would leave her more time to write.

Her fingers clenched. That was the reason she could never marry him. He would not allow her to become a published author — he had made that perfectly clear last night. Not even for the well-being of the children and her own comfort would she give up her determination to achieve her goal. If only she had not injured her ankle, she could have set out for London immediately. However, that excursion would have to wait until she was able to walk normally.

Two journeymen touched their caps

as they wandered past on their way to collect their gardening tools. There was the sound of voices coming from the stable yard, and the kitchen door opened and shut a couple of times. Her staff were up, and about their duties — she hadn't realised just how early they began their day. She couldn't see the need for this, as there was no urgency for anything to be done at the crack of dawn. She would speak to the housekeeper upon this subject and ensure that in future no one was obliged to start their day so early unless they wished to.

The bandage on her ankle had meant she could not wear a shoe on that foot, and she would have to consider what she could do about this before her visitor arrived.

'Good morning, miss; the kettle is singing, and there's plenty of bread from yesterday. I can toast some and bring you something out here.' A smiling maid dipped in a curtsy.

'That would be wonderful, thank

you. And some of that delicious strawberry conserve to go with the toast, if that is not too much trouble. This morning I would prefer coffee rather than chocolate. I shall make my way around to the terrace, so please bring my breakfast there.'

She had just heard the church clock in the village strike eight times when the unmistakable sound of a horse approaching made her start. Surely the wretched man could not be coming at this hour? Even he must know visiting so early was unacceptable.

Then she relaxed as the young doctor came into view. She was glad she had had the foresight to place her injured limb on a chair so it was elevated as she had been instructed. He raised his hand in greeting and she responded. He trotted around to the back to leave his horse, and then joined her.

'What are you doing down here, Miss Sinclair? I thought I gave you strict instructions to remain upstairs?'

'I could not stay indoors on such a

beautiful morning. I hope you will join me for coffee and toast?'

'I should be delighted, but first I will take a look at your ankle.' He looked unnaturally serious. 'I don't know if you are aware of this, but it was the fact that the duke did not rest after his leg was set that aggravated his injury, causing him to be in pain and find walking all but impossible.'

'Mr Digby told me, but I believe that was not the only reason for his trouble. I gather his leg had not been set correctly, either. I appreciate your concern, sir, but my ankle is merely sprained, so the two cases are not in any way alike.'

He did not look critically impressed by this statement, but made no comment. Instead, he flicked aside her skirts and expertly prodded and poked her ankle. She winced a couple of times but made no sound.

'You do not appear to have done it any serious harm by your unnecessary exertions, Miss Sinclair. Whatever your feelings on the matter, it will heal much quicker if you do as I suggest.'

'I shall remain here until the sun comes around and makes it uncomfortably hot — then I shall recline on the *chaise longue* in the drawing room. However, what I will not do is remain in my apartment.'

'Then I must be satisfied with that. I am going to call on his grace now: I have a feeling that he overdid it yesterday, and might well be feeling the consequences today.'

After sharing her breakfast, he took his leave. She had expected him to enquire after the well-being of Viola, but he had said nothing; perhaps he was not interested in her friend in a romantic way after all.

★   ★   ★

When a nervous footman announced that Dr Adams had come to see him, Everett frowned. The last thing he wanted was for his physician to tell him to slow down, and not to go and see Lydia for a second time.

'Send him in; have coffee brought.' He had barely had time to position himself on a comfortable chair — as if he had been sitting reading a journal, and not pacing about the study lost in thought — when the young man strolled in.

'Good morning, your grace. I wish to apologise for leaving without speaking to you last night. Miss Sinclair had only sprained her ankle, nothing more serious, and so I departed without coming back into the house.'

He obviously didn't know anything about the excursion in the middle of the night, and Everett decided it should remain a secret between himself and Lydia — no, that wasn't correct, for the children were in on it too.

'Thank you for taking time to call in and inform me. I am riding over there myself shortly, as I have had some news from Mr Digby that I must give her.'

The doctor flipped aside his coat-tails

and sat down. 'It was a thoroughly enjoyable occasion last night, your grace, I much appreciated been included on your guest list. I found Miss Carstairs delightful company, and intend to further my acquaintance with her.'

Everett wasn't accustomed to talking about such things. His parents hadn't discussed personal feelings and thoughts with each other, let alone their sons. His role had been to behave impeccably at all times, and not to show the slightest emotion — however upset or unwell he might be. He had been severely punished if he transgressed and broke the strict rules of etiquette and protocol that had ruled his family for generations.

He poured himself a cup of coffee from the silver jug and sipped it thoughtfully. He was the Duke of Hemingford now, and could do anything he damn well pleased. When the children came to live with him, they would not be forced to abide by the strict regime he and his brother had suffered. He would allow them to run free as they were doing now, to enjoy their life; and he would never inflict physical chastisement on any of them, however dire their behaviour. As long as they were polite and worked hard at their schoolbooks, he would be satisfied.

'We have heard from an uncle of the children that he wishes to take them from me and bring them up himself, as he is a closer blood relative than I. He will do so over my dead body. I know I didn't want them initially, but in the short time they have been here, I have come to enjoy their company and wish to get to know them better.'

'Is your man applying to the court to have you made their legal guardian? I can't see any judge in the land being willing to hand them over when they are already in the care of a duke.'

'Yes, he's taking care of things, as he always does. A little over two months ago, I had almost given up — was contemplating taking the easy way out.

Much has changed in so short a time — and all because of your intervention.'

'I'm happy to be of service, your grace, but I rather think you would have adapted to your circumstances once Miss Sinclair and the children came into your life.'

'I wish you to call me Hemingford, for I now count you as a friend. I will tell you in the strictest confidence that I intend to marry Lydia Sinclair at the earliest possible opportunity. I take it you intend to do the same with the governess?'

The young man looked somewhat startled by his announcement. 'I had not thought that far ahead — I've only met her once. Indeed, are you quite sure you are not being a trifle precipitate? I would have thought you would need rather more than three weeks to make such an important decision.'

14

Lydia had given her word to Dr Adams not to go upstairs until she retired; therefore, she would have to see his grace dressed as she was in her simple morning gown. Beth had attended her in the drawing room and rearranged her hair in a more becoming style, but she could hardly change her gown anywhere but in the privacy of her dressing room.

'Aunt Lydia, Miss Carstairs said we are not to mention what happened last night to anyone, and especially not to the twins. Why is that?' The boy was genuinely puzzled by this. Richard and Emma had been given a short break from their studies, and had chosen to come in to see their aunt rather than rush about outside as they usually did.

'The duke is a very important man,

Richard, and people might think his behaviour quite extraordinary. We have no wish to cause him any embarrassment, have we?'

The boy shook his head. 'I remember once when Mama and Papa were home that he went off in the middle of the night to see someone. Mama said it was because he was in his cups — but I don't know what that meant.'

His sister explained it to him. 'It means that he had taken too much alcohol, Richard. Gentlemen like to do this quite a lot.'

'Good heavens!' Lydia exclaimed. 'Whoever told you that, Emma?'

'I heard Mrs Turnbull saying it after church last week. I didn't mean to eavesdrop, but she does have rather a loud voice.'

Lydia smiled at the girl. 'You are quite right to say so, my love. I don't think we need worry ourselves about such things; in my experience, most gentlemen are very well behaved.'

They kept glancing out of the

window, and she realised they were hoping to see the duke during their short period of recreation.

'You must run along now, Miss Carstairs will be expecting you. I shall send word when his grace arrives, as I'm sure he will wish to speak to you.'

'We like him a lot, Aunt Lydia. We didn't when we first met him, you know. We think he's a jolly good fellow.'

'Richard is right; now he is able to get about easily, he's not dark and grumpy all the time.'

The children scampered off, happy to do so now they knew they wouldn't miss seeing their new friend when he came. She had yet to come up with a set of questions that wouldn't sound presumptuous. She could hardly ask him if his intentions were honourable or if he wished to make her his mistress.

Was it possible he had been bosky? That would account for his visit, at least. But from what the children had told her — and they had repeated it several times in great detail — he had not shown the slightest signs of inebriation.

Her niece was right to say the duke was a changed man. Could it be that his curmudgeonly behaviour had been caused by his inability to get about the place? An active gentleman would not enjoy being restricted as he had been before Dr Adams had reset his leg.

She was still trying to formulate her approach when he arrived in person. He strode in as if he owned the place — which, of course, he did — nodded casually, gave her a heart-stopping smile, and dropped into the nearest chair as if he belonged there.

'Good morning. I know you told me to present myself this afternoon, but I could not remain away as I have something urgent I wish to tell you.'

'Then please feel free to speak, your grace, it must be something important to bring you here so early in the day.' She glanced pointedly at the clock, which showed it was scarcely ten minutes past ten o'clock.

He refused to be rebuffed by her remark, stretching out his long, booted legs and folding his arms across his chest. This gesture drew her eyes to his torso and she could not help but notice that he was a fine figure of a man.

'Digby tells me the children have an uncle. What do you know about this fellow?'

'I know that my brother-in-law did have a younger sibling — they were estranged — I never met him and he was never spoken of.' A feeling of dread made her stomach lurch. 'Is this man coming to take the children away from us?'

Before she could protest, he was beside her, and took her hands in his. 'Don't look so stricken, sweetheart, you have nothing to worry about. I wish you and the children to move to Hemingford Court — you should have been with me from the beginning. It was most remiss of me to have not taken you in when I first heard about your plight.'

Her head was spinning, but there was

one thing she did understand. 'If we will be safe from this man, then we will move immediately.'

'I don't think there's any need to come today, my dear, I wish to get the nursery floor refurbished and redecorated before you move in.'

'You're right, I am being silly. I have several loyal and able outside men, and they can prevent anything untoward from occurring until we can transfer to the big house.' He was rather too close, and his proximity was making her feel unsettled. 'Could I ask you to return to your seat, please, your grace? It is not seemly for you to be where you are.'

To her relief he didn't argue, but regained his feet and took his earlier place. 'I expect the children are full of my visit last night, and I must apologise for disrupting your household . . . ' He paused and looked away. There was something else going on here, something she didn't quite understand.

'I expect you know how my parents and brother died. I was just falling asleep when I realised that I hadn't spoken to the doctor, that I hadn't seen him again after he left with you. I had visions of there having been a dreadful accident and of you all lying injured in a ditch somewhere.'

For a second, her heart went out to him and she believed his explanation. Then she became aware his shoulders were shaking — he was laughing.

'You wretch; you almost had me believing your nonsense. The children think you must have been drunk, and I think that a far more likely explanation.'

'Then shall we settle for that as a reason?'

'And will speak of it no more. When do you want us to remove to your home? I expect it will take at least a week to get the nursery floor ready for occupation.'

'As I intend to send a further half-dozen men to work on the much-needed repairs and renewals to this house, you will be well protected. I should like to see you tomorrow — why don't you and the children come and inspect what will be your future home?'

'Emma and Richard are hoping to see you today. There are two things I must ask you to do before they come down. The first is to not refer to this uncle who is looking for them; the second, to desist from using endearments when you speak to me. It will give them the wrong impression.'

'I agree with the first, and have no difficulty with that. However, sweetheart, I refer to you affectionately because I consider you as one of my young charges. The children will accept it as such, and so must you.'

'In which case, your grace, I shall say no more on that subject either.' She bit her lip to try and hold back what she dearly wanted to say. All would have been well if he hadn't then smiled in an irritating way.

'I cannot tell you what a relief it is to me, your grace,' she informed him mischievously, 'to be considered in the same way as the children. You are so much older than I am that I consider you as an older relative — as an uncle I suppose.'

His eyes darkened, and he pushed himself out of his chair and was looming over her before she had time to protest. Her breath caught in her throat and her bodice became unaccountably tighter.

*   *   *

An uncle, indeed! The way he felt about Lydia had nothing to do with being a relative, and everything to do with being a lover. He was beside her without conscious thought; and, as he watched, her eyes widened and her cheeks flushed becomingly.

He was about to show just how he thought of her when the children burst in and the moment was gone. He turned with a friendly smile, and to his astonishment they threw themselves into his arms.

'We are so glad to see you, your

grace, but didn't expect you until this afternoon.' Emma clung to his hand whilst Richard leaned his head trustingly against him. His arms moved of their own volition until he was embracing them both.

'Good morning, little ones, I'm delighted to see you. Shall we go outside and throw a stick for Benji, and leave your aunt to rest?'

With his arms around their shoulders, he gently pushed them in the direction of the exit; he turned as he reached the door. As he'd expected, she was still staring at him. 'This discussion is not ended; we will resume it as soon as can be arranged. By the by, in future I shall be referring to you as Lydia and you may call me Hemingford.'

Richard tugged at his coat. 'We should like to call you Uncle, but don't know your given name.'

His sister nodded. 'Shall we address you as Uncle Hemingford?'

'No, I think not. Uncle Everett will do much better.'

He spent a happy half-hour playing with all four children as the nursemaids came to join them with the twins. He decided it wasn't his place to tell them they would soon be moving from the Dower House — he would leave Lydia to explain it to them.

On his return, he sought out Digby and the secretary. They were busy writing letters in their own domain. Both men resided at the Court — the secretary had a chamber somewhere upstairs, and Digby a small apartment in the guest wing.

'No, don't get up, I have come with a suggestion. I should like you both to move to the Dower House when Miss Sinclair and the children come here. The house is in good shape, and you will be far more comfortable there.'

'If you are quite sure, your grace, my nephew and I would be delighted to accept your kind offer.' Digby was on his feet and beaming.

Everett hadn't known the young man was Digby's nephew — he should have done. In future, he would take more interest in his employees.

'I've not told the children, I'm leaving that to Miss Sinclair. However, they will be here sometime tomorrow to look around the house, and I'm hoping once they see it they will be happy to move.'

'I should think they will, your grace. The Dower House is all very well, but to live at Hemingford Court will be an improvement.'

'From the racket coming from the nursery floor, I take it the workmen are already busy up there.'

'Indeed they are, your grace; everything will be ready in a week. Presumably the nursemaids, governess, and Miss Sinclair's personal maid will accompany them. Are we to retain the remaining staff for our use?'

'Good God, man, you will need more than a few women and the housekeeper if you are to live comfortably. All household expenses are to be paid from my account — consider it part of your wages. I should think you should have a butler and at least one footman — you will also need two riding horses, and a team to pull a carriage. In fact, do whatever you like — it's your home now.'

They both looked rather stunned by his largesse; he rather liked being able to improve the lot of the people that were close to him. 'You must choose your horses from my stables or stud.'

He strolled away, and for some strange reason everywhere he looked seemed brighter and more pleasing than it had done before. This was decidedly strange, and one couldn't put this down to fresh paint or newly scrubbed floors. Then he understood. For the first time in his life, he was happy.

* * *

Lydia decided to tell the older children why they were going to visit Hemingford. They were delighted at the prospect of moving in with their new best friend — Uncle Everett, as they were now to call him.

'It will be much better there, we will have more room to run around,' Emma said as they stepped into the phaeton which had arrived to collect them.

'You have more than enough room here — three times the space you have ever had before! However, I think the duke will be a good influence on you both. Sometimes I think I allow you too much leeway, and a little more discipline will not go amiss.'

For a moment the two children looked disconcerted, but then rallied. 'Uncle Everett is a capital fellow; he won't expect us to behave any differently,' Richard announced blithely.

She exchanged an anxious glance with her friend. Viola and she had discussed the possibility that the children would have to behave differently when they were living under his roof. Although there was no danger he would use physical punishment, they might well discover they had to stick to more rules than they had previously been accustomed to.

Travelling in this carriage with four children and three adults was somewhat overcrowded, but the journey was mercifully short. She was sure they would not suffer unduly even though it was unpleasantly warm today. She had her walking sticks with her, and had become an expert in their use.

'I shall not accompany you around the house, children, Miss Carstairs will do so. I shall wait for you on the terrace.'

She had expected the carriage to stop at the rear of the building, but this time it bowled around to the front. Here they were met by the duke himself, plus a positive army of liveried retainers. So much splendour silenced the older children, and even the twins were quiet.

Then he bounded down the marble steps and snatched first Emma and then Richard from the carriage, swinging them around so they squealed with delight.

'Us too, us too,' the twins yelled in chorus, and he willingly obliged.

'I think we had better descend immediately, Viola, in case his grace wishes to treat us in the same manner.' Lydia found getting out more difficult than getting in, and she was relieved to be on the ground before the duke could pick her up.

He'd observed their rapid descent and laughed out loud. She could not prevent her heart skipping a beat. Whatever his faults — and they were legion — he really was a charming gentleman when he put his mind to it.

The children did not seem to think it odd that she was introduced to the butler and the housekeeper, and that they, along with the other assembled servants, curtsied and bowed. However, her friend was smiling in a particular way which sent warning signals up and down Lydia's spine. The duke could have introduced her in this manner because she was going to be a member of the household, almost a member of the family, but Viola obviously thought it indicated something else entirely. Lydia shook her head in warning, but her friend just smiled in a knowing manner.

★ ★ ★

The children pronounced themselves delighted with what would be their new accommodation the following week, and then asked permission to visit the maze.

'You may go, children, as long as Miss Carstairs and the nursemaids are with you. Don't forget to take a flag in so you can wave it if you become lost.'

Richard put his hands on his hips and looked rather serious. 'I don't think that will be much good, Aunt Lydia, as there's nobody around who knows the way out.'

'Benji does, so make sure you have him with you.'

Viola turned as if about to say something, but Lydia forestalled her.

'Not a word from you, Miss Carstairs. I'm finding everything decidedly confusing this morning, and don't require any comments from you on the subject.'

The children trooped off accompanied by their carers, leaving her at the mercy of her host. He pounced as soon as she was alone. 'Come with me if you please, Miss Sinclair, there is something most particular I wish to speak to you about.' He gestured towards her sticks. 'I have my bath chair you can use, if you would prefer.'

'No, thank you; as you can see I am perfectly capable of making my own way with the help of these sticks.'

Reluctantly, she allowed herself to be guided along a wide passageway, and into what could only be his private sanctum: his study. She was about to tell him to leave the door open when she heard it click closed behind her.

'I'm not going to ravish you, my love, so don't look so terrified. I merely want to speak to you without anyone overhearing what I have to say.'

Hearing her wild thoughts put into words was enough to release the tension. 'I do not trust you to behave yourself, your grace . . . '

His eyes flashed a warning. 'I believe I told you to call me Hemingford in future.'

She smiled sweetly. 'I believe you did, but I prefer to call you Uncle Everett as the children do. More appropriate considering the age difference, don't you think?'

This had been a remarkably foolish thing to say, as his eyes took on a predatory gleam and he closed the distance between them in two long strides.

Her heart was pounding so loudly she was surprised he couldn't hear it. He was no more than a hand's breadth from her. His heat was pulsing from him. Her hands became slippery and she lost her grip on the handles of her canes. Inadvertently, she put her weight on her bad leg — which gave way, and she began to crumple.

15

Everett caught her as she fell. He cursed himself for frightening her and almost causing her to have another accident.

'Here, let me carry you to a seat.' She weighed less than he expected for a young woman of her height and build. He placed her tenderly on the sofa, then stepped away so she did not feel threatened.

'Thank you, Hemingford, I am not as steady as I thought.'

He took a seat several yards from her before replying. 'I intend to make you my wife, Lydia. I suggest you become accustomed to the idea.'

He thought she might go pale, shake her head, cry out . . . but she did something else entirely. She laughed at him.

'My word, that must be the most

unromantic proposal any young lady has ever received. My response, Hemingford, is no. You must become accustomed to not always having your own way. I told you when we first met that I have no wish to marry you or anyone else, and I still hold to that opinion.'

'Your opinion is irrelevant, sweetheart, Hemingford men always get their own way in the end. I shall not coerce you, but I promise you that once you are under my roof, you will change your mind. I know you have feelings for me . . . '

She raised a hand. 'I desire you, that is true, but that is quite different from wishing to have you as a husband. I know I would become a duchess and want for nothing . . . but those things are of no matter to me. If ever I do give up my independence, it will be to a man I am in love with. I might be an innocent, but I know the difference between lust and love, even if you don't.'

He was shocked by her comment. His knowledge of young ladies was not wide, but he was sure a well-brought-up girl would never have dared to say such a thing.

'Admit it, Hemingford, you no more love me than I do you. Your senses are engaged for the first time in many years, and you're feeling like a red-blooded gentleman. Might I suggest that you get yourself a mistress? That would be so much easier for both of us.'

He had heard quite enough of this unsuitable conversation. 'You are impertinent, miss, and would do better to hold your tongue.' He saw a look of what could only be triumph flit across her face. The lump that had unaccountably wedged in his chest at her appalling conversation vanished. The girl had deliberately provoked him in the only way she knew in order to get him to retract his proposal.

'Why would I wish to dine elsewhere when I have plenty to eat at home?' For a moment, she looked puzzled at his analogy, but then her cheeks turned scarlet as she grasped his meaning.

'I will not be your wife, and neither will I be your mistress, sir. The children may reside with you, but I shall remain where I am.'

'I'm afraid that will not be possible, my dear, as Mr Digby and his nephew will be moving into the Dower House next week. You have no option but to come here or be homeless.'

Her head dropped, and he felt a brute for being so harsh. It had been a long time since he had spoken to a young lady, and he had never come close to proposing. He had a lot of fences to mend before she could forgive his clumsy offer — but he was determined to woo her over the next few weeks until she was as irrevocably in love with him as he was with her.

He had no intention of burdening her with his feelings until he was sure she reciprocated them. If, after a month or two, she was still adamant she would not have him, then he would have to let her go. He would never force her into a union with him, however much he would like to do so.

'Lydia, sweetheart, shall we pretend this conversation never took place? Forget what I said about marriage; I will not bother you with the subject until you are ready to hear it.'

She raised her head and he was horrified to see tears glinting in her eyes. 'I thank you, but what has been said can never be forgotten. I think it might be better if I lived elsewhere. The Dower House is more than big enough to accommodate Mr Digby, his nephew, and myself. Now, he *is* like an uncle to me; I'm sure we will deal famously together.'

Now was not the time to force the issue. 'If that's what you want, then so be it. Do you wish me to speak to him, or will you do that yourself?'

'Perhaps you would be kind enough to ask him to come and see me here? I believe that our conversation is over. I'm sure the children would be delighted to see you outside at the maze.'

He bit back a sharp retort. He was not accustomed to being dismissed from his own house in such a cavalier fashion. He stood, nodded, and strode out without replying. She could stew for a bit, and not know whether he had actually conveyed her message or not.

He was waylaid by one of the nursemaids who requested that he go and retrieve the children from the centre of the maze. The wretched dog had led them in and then vanished, leaving them marooned in there. When eventually everyone had been collected, he had completely forgotten he had been asked to fetch Digby.

★　★　★

Lydia waited for half an hour, and then decided that either Mr Digby wasn't available, or Hemingford hadn't bothered to convey her message. There was little point in sitting here on her own in his study; she could either join the children in the garden, or ask for the carriage to be brought round so she could return in solitary splendour.

She decided on the latter; the phaeton was waiting at the side of the house, where she had instructed it to go when she hopped out.

'Please take me home; then come back immediately to collect the children, Miss Carstairs, and the nursemaid.'

As the distance between her and her tormentor increased, she began to feel more sanguine, to believe that matters might work out eventually. She was certain that if she continued to refuse him, he would eventually give up and find himself someone more amenable. She didn't consider herself an unsuitable bride for a duke: after all, she was the granddaughter of an earl, and although impoverished, she was well-educated and passably pretty.

She might have felt differently about his casual proposal if he had said he was head over heels in love with her.

Being married because the gentleman wished to share her bed was not a good start to any union, in her opinion. If the couple did not have love to bind them, then what would happen when the passion faded? They would both be left in a bond that was unsatisfactory.

If she was to separate herself from the children in order to keep away from him, then she could not rely on his financial support. This made it imperative she found herself a publisher who would actually pay her for her work.

The second novel was already two chapters long, and she intended to take this with her to London as well. If she could show that she was a serious writer who would produce an annual book, then she was certain she was more likely to secure a favourable outcome.

When she was home, she went straight to the study and wrote four letters — one to each of the publishers she had selected as a possible recipient of her opus. She folded, sealed, and addressed each missive, then rang the bell.

'I wish to have these taken to the village and put on the mail coach. One of the grooms can do this, and they can ride the little mare or the cob.' The maid curtsied, and took the folded squares and the necessary coins to pay for their delivery.

Satisfied she had set things in motion, Lydia returned to her apartment. Travelling on her bottom was slow and undignified, but meant she could safely negotiate the stairs in either direction.

She had indicated in the letters that she would be in London by the end of the week. Doctor Adams had said her ankle should be mended in a day or two, and she hoped that was the case. She had no wish to hobble about the streets like an old lady. This would hardly give a good impression to any gentleman she hoped to persuade to publish her book, and to pay her a reasonable recompense for so doing.

Beth would have to be taken into her confidence as she could not go alone to Town. Even with a maid at her side, she was still bending the rules; but as she had no wish to conform, and cared little if her reputation was damaged, she would do as she pleased.

'Will we be staying overnight, miss? I'd dearly love to see some of the sights, as I've not been to London in my life.'

'I had not intended to, Beth, but I see no reason why we shouldn't. There are some perfectly respectable places we could stay at. I intend to travel on the first coach in the morning, and complete my business by mid-afternoon. This would leave us the remainder of the day and the following morning to see the sights. I'm sure you understand that I have no wish for anyone else to know where we're going.'

Her maid nodded. 'As you only have one copy of your book, miss, how can you show it to all four gentlemen?'

'I intend to give them the first two chapters of my next novel — I have already copied out those chapters four times. Then, I shall leave them to read it for half an hour, and return for their answer. I'm hoping that the first person I speak to will be so pleased with what he has read that he will offer me a contract immediately. However, I doubt that will be the case, and I might well have to visit all four gentlemen before I find a home for my book. That is why it might take me most of the day.'

She had decided against informing her friend of her intentions, as she was certain Viola would try and stop her. Although they had talked about Lydia's aspirations to be a novelist, she didn't think they had been taken seriously.

The older children had postponed their morning schoolwork in order to go on the excursion, so when they returned they had to go straight upstairs to get on with their studies. This meant that their governess was also occupied, which suited Lydia perfectly.

They did not meet again until the

children were getting ready for bed, and Lydia had come to tell them a bedtime story. 'I'm going to eat in my sitting room, Viola, I have been up and down stairs more than enough times today.'

'Shall I join you?'

'If you don't mind, I shall retire early, so it might be better if you dine in your own sitting room tonight. We can catch up with your news tomorrow morning.'

The next two days passed uneventfully, and Lydia was relieved that her friend had only wished to discuss how things would be managed when they moved the following week. There had been no mention of Hemingford at all. Of course, no one else knew about the proposal, or that they had parted on bad terms, so there was only the matter of their unusual welcome. This, Lydia was able to dismiss as nothing untoward, and the subject was closed.

On the day of her trip to Town, she and Beth were up with the lark, and crept out of the house like burglars at first light. The groom, who had also been sworn to secrecy, was waiting with the pony cart to transport them to the village.

'I do not require you to return today, Bertie, I shall send word to the house when I need to be collected. Make sure you mention nothing about my trip. I've no wish to be the subject of gossip amongst the staff.' She gave the young man a silver coin, and he was well satisfied with the exchange.

She had written a note to Viola explaining why she had gone, that she would be staying overnight and expected to return late the following day. No doubt her friend would think of some-thing suitable to tell the children — there was no need for Hemingford to know anything about it.

The duke had not visited himself, but there were now several extra outside men busy in the garden. Mr Digby had also been absent, so she had not yet had the opportunity to inform him she intended to remain where she was, and that he would not have the house to himself after all.

The coach arrived punctually; there was no time for the passengers already on board to get out, and barely time for her and her maid to get in, before the horses were changed and the vehicle was on the move again. She had her precious manuscript in a brown paper parcel on her lap, and Beth had their overnight things in a valise.

Having got up so early, they'd not had time to break their fast and were pleased to be able to disembark at the next stop and find some refreshments. When she dipped into her reticule for the necessary coins to pay for this, she saw to her horror the note she had written for Viola was still contained therein. She had forgotten to leave it on the breakfast table as she had intended.

*   *   *

Everett had been shocked, but not surprised, when he had discovered Lydia had gone home. He had behaved badly, but would allow her a day or two to recover her temper before he attempted to put things right. He did, however, remember to tell Digby about the new arrangements.

'I shall be delighted to have Miss Sinclair living with me, your grace. I think it an excellent notion — a young lady cannot be too careful about her reputation.'

Until that moment, Everett had not even considered the possible ramifications of having an eligible girl living under his roof. Miss Carstairs was also single, but she was an employee, so didn't count in the eyes of society.

'I asked her to marry me, Digby, but she laughed and turned me down. It ended badly, and I'm staying away for a day or two in order to allow her to recover her temper. I intend to do my best to court her, but now she is to live elsewhere this is going to be more difficult.'

'You have every right to visit me when I move, your grace, and cannot help but see her when you do so. Also, she will want to see the children every day, will she not?'

'I hope so. Which reminds me, have you had any news about this uncle?'

'Not yet, your grace, but I assure you I will bring the information to you as soon as I get it. I've already lodged the necessary papers at the High Court, and your legal guardianship will be confirmed long before this person arrives to make a nuisance of himself. I'm sure I can pay him off — he only became interested after he discovered they were under your protection.'

'I'm damned if I will give him a penny. If he does appear, keep him away from the children at all costs. I don't wish any of them to be upset. I consider them as Hemingfords now. They are part of my family, and a very welcome part at that.'

On the third day, he rode over to the Dower House mid-morning to find the place in uproar. He dismounted and flung the reins to a waiting stableboy.

He strode in to find the governess weeping in the drawing room. 'What is all the fuss about? Tell me at once, Miss Carstairs, what is going on here?'

'Thank God you're here, your grace, we cannot find Lydia or her maid anywhere. She has run away. She must have left in the middle of the night, and we have no idea where she might have gone.'

His gut twisted and he swallowed bile. This was his fault — he had driven her away. The thought of the woman he loved to distraction wandering about somewhere, without funds and with no gentleman to protect her, filled him with horror.

'You are distressing the children with your fuss. I suggest you pull yourself together and set them a proper example. Have you spoken to any of the outside men?'

'I spoke to the head groom but he knows nothing about it.'

'Then I shall do so myself.' He turned to the crying children. 'There's no need to be upset, little ones. I shall bring your aunt home safe, I give you my word.'

It didn't take long to discover that Lydia had been taken to the coaching inn; the fact that the boy had not been required to return to collect them today filled him with dread. This was far worse than he had first thought.

He dashed back inside and informed the governess he was going to London to find Lydia and fetch her home. Then he urged his horse into a flat gallop, and was back in his apartment, shouting for his valet to pack him an overnight bag, within ten minutes of leaving the Dower House.

'I shall travel post — there's no need for you to accompany me. However, I wish the travelling carriage to set out for London as soon as I have left. It must go to Grosvenor Square. I shall take Miss Sinclair there when I find her. Have someone go immediately to the Dower House and pack a trunk for her. Bring this with you.'

Whilst he had been giving his orders, he had stripped and changed into something more elegant than his country attire. He had a second wardrobe at his town house, so there was no necessity for him to take a bag with him. He had a wallet full of flimsies and a velvet bag full of gold guineas — that would be more than enough for his expenses.

His gig was waiting outside with Bates sitting on the box.

'I shall drive; we will get there quicker if I do. You can return with this vehicle at a more decorous pace.'

In a little over an hour from when he had first heard the dreadful news, he was sitting in the back of a post-chaise racing towards London. He would have ample opportunity on the journey of two hours to think about his plan of action. He knew for a certainty that Lydia and her maid had boarded the stage at five, and exactly where they could disembark. However, if they were not going to Town but getting off at one of the stops in between, he might well miss her.

In order to avoid this possibility, he instructed the driver to enquire — at every stop they made to change the team — if a young lady and her maid had got down there.

Finally, confident his quarry had not left the coach at any stage between the village and London itself, he paid the exorbitant sum for his journey without a qualm — he would pay a hundred times more in order to recover his beloved.

He had no need to announce his pedigree: it was obvious that he was a gentleman of importance and therefore he received the attention and respect he was accustomed to.

The busy inn had already had several stagecoaches terminated there, but this was no obstacle to him. Everett found a willing assistant in a young groom and sent him around to make enquiries. The lad came back with the best news possible.

'Two young ladies fitting your description, my lord, ordered a hackney carriage to take them to Fulbright Street.'

He tossed the boy a coin and set off on foot. Lydia did not know the city as he did. The destination she had enquired about was no more than a mile away if you took a direct route. He could be there in less than half an hour.

*   *   *

'Here we are — there, this is where I must go first.'

Her maid viewed the entrance with suspicion. 'It doesn't look very grand, miss; are you sure this is the right place?'

'I am. I wish now I had made a firm appointment and was not just arriving on the day I stated in my letter of introduction. I did say I would be coming this morning, but I've no idea if the gentleman I wish to see, one Mr Jonathan Peabody, will actually be here — or, indeed, will wish to see me at all.'

She stiffened her spine and marched up the steps. Inside was as unprepossessing as the outside, and she almost turned around and walked out. A shrivelled individual dressed in faded black was sitting behind a table. He didn't appear to have the energy to stand up, but almost managed it. 'Can I be of assistance, miss?'

'I have an appointment with Mr Peabody this morning. Kindly inform him that I am here.'

He shuffled off through a door behind him, leaving her standing in the dusty vestibule regretting her decision with every minute that passed. Then the elderly gentleman returned.

'Mr Peabody is too busy to see you, miss; if you would care to leave your manuscript, he will read it when he has a moment.'

This was almost a relief, as Lydia was sure she didn't wish to be associated with anyone who worked in such dismal surroundings. She put down her parcel, undid the string, and carefully opened it. She extracted one of the smaller bundles which contained the first two chapters to her future book, and placed it on the counter. 'I shall leave this partial of my next novel, which should be sufficient for Mr Peabody to make up his mind. The details he requires in order to contact me are with it.'

She turned and swept out, not waiting for him to make any sort of response. There was no point in waiting half an hour to see if he did actually look at it, as she was certain it would only go in his wastepaper basket.

'Now, we can walk to our next destination, as it is only a short distance from here according to the driver of the hackney carriage.' They set off briskly, and the next publishers looked a much more interesting proposition. The building was freshly painted, there was a brass plate on the wall announcing it as a publishing house, and when she asked Beth to knock on the door it was opened immediately by a smiling and smart young man.

'Good morning to you, Miss Sinclair, Mr Dunwoody is expecting you.' They were ushered in, and the interior was as pleasing as the exterior.

'Mr Dunwoody will see you in this chamber after he has had time to look at your manuscript. I shall have refreshments sent in to you, and there are several interesting journals to read whilst you wait.'

Lydia put the parcel on the polished sideboard and handed over her chapters with more enthusiasm than she had done the previous time.

'These are the opening chapters for my next book — I believe that Mr Dunwoody might find it useful to have a shorter piece of my writing to look at initially.'

The young man nodded and smiled. 'Exactly so, Miss Sinclair. An excellent idea, and one he will appreciate, I'm sure. However, I should like to take the entire manuscript as well, if you don't mind?'

With her precious book in his hands,

he dashed off. For the first time, she thought that perhaps this might be the start of her career as a published author. She could have posted the manuscript to him under a masculine pseudonym, but she had made the decision some time ago to pursue her career under her own name, whatever the consequences.

There was no clock in the small antechamber, and despite having been served with freshly brewed coffee and almond biscuits, the time dragged. Beth had happily settled herself in a corner and was perusing a copy of *La Belle Assemblée* whilst Lydia paced anxiously.

Was it a good sign that he was taking so long to make a decision? Her heart was fluttering in her chest like a caged bird, and the more time that passed, the more anxious she became.

Then the door was flung open and a small round gentleman, with a florid complexion and a scarlet waistcoat, burst in. 'My dear Miss Sinclair, I do apologise for keeping you waiting so long! I became so engrossed in your work that I had no idea of the time.'

'You like it?'

'Indeed I do. Would you care to come into my office so we can discuss business matters?'

There was no need to take her maid with her; it was far too late to worry about breaking any further rules. He stood aside and flapped his arms, indicating she should go in front of him. His office was the other side of the vestibule, and was tidy, clean and well appointed.

The young man pulled out a chair for her and she took it. Mr Dunwoody resumed his seat behind his desk. She didn't think she'd ever been so happy in her life. Her dream was about to come true, and she would be in a position to support herself once the contract was signed.

Then she saw her complete manuscript on a side table. It was sitting there, apparently unopened, which was a puzzle. Even the slowest reader — and one must assume that a publisher was not one of those people — could have read the two sample chapters in half the time that she had been kept waiting.

Her smile faded and her optimism drained away. The two chapters were on the desk, but these looked as if they had been barely glanced at. What was going on here?

'Miss Sinclair, I would really like to publish your book. It is quite the most excellent story I have read in a long while. However, you must understand that as a debut author, one cannot guarantee you will sell sufficient copies to cover the costs. Therefore, because I am so enthusiastic about your writing, I'm prepared to offer you a special deal.'

'You wish me to pay for the publication of my book myself?'

He beamed at her. 'That is exactly right, Miss Sinclair.'

'In which case, Mr Dunwoody, I

thank you for your time and bid you good day. I'm not interested in an arrangement of that sort.'

With her precious papers safely returned to her, she stalked out of the charlatan's office. Small wonder the place looked so prosperous — they made their money out of gullible authors desperate to see their work in print, and prepared to pay whatever they were asked in order to do so.

'Beth, we have been duped, and wasted most of the morning here. Please help me to tie my parcel up again. Our next destination is too far to walk, so we must try and attract a hackney carriage.'

The parcel was heavy in her arms. It could not have changed its weight, but it certainly felt more cumbersome than it had when she set off in such high spirits so many hours ago.

'Never mind, miss, at least we had something nice to eat and drink.'

The third place that they visited refused even to allow them entry. She was turned away as if she was of no account, and this infuriated her. The final office was a brisk twenty minutes' walk away, and she used this time to recover her temper. She now had no expectation at all of finding her manuscript a home.

'I have no wish to go in myself this time. Just take the entire parcel and give it to someone. I no longer care whether anyone wishes to read it or not. We shall then find ourselves some overnight accommodation, and go and see the sights.'

Her maid wasn't gone long. 'There was no one to hand it to, miss, so I left it on the desk. I'm ever so excited to be staying in a hotel tonight. Are we going to the one the driver mentioned?'

'We might as well, as I have no knowledge of anywhere else. I'm sure we passed the building on our walk here, so can retrace our steps easily enough.'

The hotel was clean and well-run, and had a small but delightful room available for the two of them. They were escorted up, and hot water and clean towels were brought immediately.

'My, miss, this is grand. Let me sponge down your spencer. Then you will look as smart as you did when we set out at dawn this morning.'

* * *

Everett arrived at his destination, but was confused as to why Lydia should wish to come here. The street was far from smart, full of rundown houses and offices, and there was nothing here he could see that could be of interest to her.

He could not help but be aware that he was attracting far too much attention. He had no idea where to go next, or from whom he could make enquiries — then he spotted an urchin pushing a barrow, and thought perhaps he might have seen something that could be of use to him.

'I saw two ladies, sir, one carrying a

large parcel, the other a valise. They went into an office a few streets from here — but I ain't sure which one it was.'

He tossed the boy a coin and set off, swinging his cane as a warning to any ne'er-do-wells who might think to accost him for his wallet.

The next street was more prosperous, and he walked along the pavement examining the polished brass plates outside to see if any one of them might be somewhere Lydia could have visited. What the hell she was doing in this part of the city, he had no idea, but it didn't seem the actions of a young lady trying to escape from the clutches of an unwanted suitor.

What about this mysterious parcel she was carrying? He stopped, lost in thought, and then something he had seen a few buildings back made everything fall into place. His darling girl was trying to find a publisher for her novel so that she could become financially independent.

He strode back to the building that had proclaimed to be the offices of Dunwoody & Ashworth, publishers of novels and poetry. It didn't take him long to discover she had left, and the reason she had done so.

He now had in his possession directions to three other possible publishing companies in the vicinity. After two unsuccessful forays, he marched into the final building.

'I wish to know if a Miss Sinclair has visited here today?'

His question caused the clerk, who was standing behind the desk, to leap into the air. 'Yes, sir, she was here earlier. Please, would you wait for a moment so that Mr Carberry may come and speak to you?'

A tall, bespectacled young man emerged, wringing his hands in his excitement. 'Miss Sinclair left her manuscript with me some time ago, but did not remain to speak to me. I have been quite engrossed by her book and believe I can offer her a contract to publish. Romantic novels are popular with my readers, but there is much more to this particular one than that.'

'I am the Duke of Hemingford. Miss Sinclair is my future wife, and she came to London without informing me. As you might imagine, Mr Carberry, I'm anxious to locate her.'

If he had expected the announcement of his name to impress the gentleman, he was disappointed. Carberry looked put out at this information.

'I take it you do not approve of her wish to become a published author. I'm not surprised that she came to see me without informing you, your grace. Am I to understand that you will refuse permission for her to have her work in the public domain where it belongs?'

Everett was about to agree when he said something else entirely. 'I have no objection to my future wife having her work published by you, Carberry. However, it must be under a pseudonym — I assume that is perfectly acceptable.'

The man was about to clap him on the shoulder but thought better of it. 'Perfectly understandable, your grace. As soon I have the name she wishes to be published under, I can draw up the contract.'

Everett nodded and bounded back down the steps, determined to find his beloved before she got herself into any further difficulties. She would have to find herself somewhere respectable to stay; there were several hotels in the area, but he was not prepared to go in and out of each making a cake of himself.

Lydia had had ample time to tidy up — but where would she go after that? He would try the Tower and the menagerie. This was the main attraction a visitor would head for upon coming to Town.

He hailed a passing hackney and gave him the instruction. When it rattled to a halt, he jumped out and called up to the driver, 'Wait for me — I shall not be long.'

As he crossed the road, he saw Lydia and her maid speaking to a red-coated Beefeater. He was at her side before she noticed his arrival.

'Lydia, my dear, I'm so glad I have caught up with you. Come, I have a carriage waiting to take you to Grosvenor Square.'

For an awful moment, he thought she was going to refuse, to make a fuss in public, but she must have seen his expression change. Instead, she nodded politely, and placed her hand on his arm when he offered it.

He assisted her into the carriage, then turned and gave her maid a handful of coins. 'Return to wherever you have reserved a room, collect your mistress's belongings, and bring them to Grosvenor Square.'

The girl curtsied, cast a worried glance in Lydia's direction, then stepped away, allowing him to close the door.

'I don't wish to have any sort of conversation with you about your behaviour or mine in so public a place.

We shall talk when we are somewhere more comfortable and private.'

Once inside the carriage, she had removed her hand as if the touch had burnt her fingers. She was now squashed in the furthest corner from him, and refused to look at him or respond to his remark.

He couldn't see her face inside the wide brim of her bonnet, and wasn't sure if she was furious or distressed by his sudden appearance. She certainly wasn't pleased — that was quite clear.

16

Lydia blinked back her tears. She should have realised he wouldn't let her achieve her dream, but instead squash any hope she had of finding herself a publisher. Then her heart sank to her boots when she recalled she had left home without telling Viola that she intended to return.

She twisted on the squabs and looked at him more closely. His face was pale, there were dark lines on either side of his nose, and he looked as if he'd not slept for weeks — which couldn't be the case.

As he had told her not to discuss anything until they reached his town house, she just handed him the note she should have left for Viola. He took it, and then became more alert when he saw to whom it was addressed. He broke the seal and read it. By the end, he looked more like himself, and smiled at her in such a way that she could not help but respond.

'You are a ninny, my darling. I should have realised you hadn't run away. I should have told you that I love you, that I shall be bereft without you at my side, but for some reason I quite forgot to say this when I proposed to you in that maladroit fashion.'

'You love me? I had no idea. I don't know what to say.'

'Then say nothing, sweetheart, until we are home.'

She settled back into her corner, averting her face so he couldn't watch her expression. Did his being in love with her make any difference? She was sure she didn't reciprocate, that her feelings were physical rather than emotional. She was not, of course, experienced in the matters of love of any sort, but being an author had caused her to study this subject in depth in other people's literary works and she considered herself an expert on the subject.

She was roused from her slumber when the duke shook her none too gently by the shoulder. 'We are here, Lydia, and I've no intention of carrying you in, so you had better wake up right away.'

Hardly a loving comment but it was sufficient to clear her head and get her ready to climb down from the hired vehicle.

The front door was opened as if by magic and she was bowed and curtsied into the enormous entrance hall. She wasn't allowed to examine her surroundings, but was hustled down numerous passageways and into the study. This was the second time she had been taken to his special chamber — she supposed he could be sure that he wouldn't be disturbed by his staff when he was there.

He closed the door with a snap behind them. 'Sit over there, Lydia, we have much to talk about.'

She did as she was told and folded her hands in her lap like a schoolgirl waiting to be castigated by an irate parent. He picked up a chair one-handed, and spun it round so he could straddle it and fold his arms along the chair back.

'I wish to tell you that the publisher, Carberry & Sons, want to publish your novel. They just need to know if you intend to use a pseudonym, or publish . . . publish under your own name. I didn't discuss what your advance would be: that is something you must ascertain for yourself when you return there to sign the contract.'

'I had intended to publish as Lydia Sinclair, but perhaps I should reconsider. What are your opinions on the matter?'

'You already know them, sweetheart. I would prefer you not to publish at all — but if it is important to you, then I will support you, whatever you decide.'

She looked up, and saw nothing but love in his eyes. Something she didn't recognise stirred inside her. 'And if I was your wife, would you allow me to continue writing under this name?'

'If you would agree to marry me, my darling, then I should be prepared to dance naked around Grosvenor Square. Allowing you to continue to write under your maiden name will be of no importance to me.'

'Then I shall hold you to that, your grace. I will marry you if you will fulfil your promise.' She was trying to repress her giggles, but not succeeding very well.

To her mortification and astonishment, he sprang to his feet, and started to remove his clothes as if they were on fire. 'No, please do not. I didn't mean . . . '

He was now down to his shirt and breeches, and about to remove his boots and stockings. He paused and looked at her. 'I'm a man of my word, darling, and I shall hold you to yours when this is done.'

Without conscious thought, she was on her feet and had moved across to him. 'Please, there's no need to continue this. I will marry you. I've no wish for you to humiliate yourself on my behalf.'

Slowly he replaced his foot on the floor and stood up so he was towering above her. 'I think you understand how I feel about you, sweetheart, I would do anything for you — I would die for you if needs be. I would much prefer it if you loved me too, but will take you on whatever terms you're prepared to offer.'

His eyes were sad and her heart went out to him. 'We are like chalk and cheese, Everett, but I think we will make a splendid couple. I don't know exactly what love is — but if it's knowing I could not spend my life without you at my side, knowing that if anything happened to you my life would be over too, then I believe I must be in love with you.'

There was a strange sound, almost like a growl, and then she was enveloped in his arms.

'If you have no objection, I shall

apply for a special licence whilst we're in Town. I doubt that I can wait until our wedding night unless it's very soon.'

'If any of your staff were to see us as we are, then both our good names would be gone.'

'Then I had better get dressed again, as your maid will be here soon with your things. Also, my valet and your trunk should be arriving as well.'

She hastily turned her back, not wishing to watch him in his disarray. The thought of how much more she would see of him when they were wed made her hot all over.

'You can turn around now, sweet-heart, I am decent again.'

She did so, and was immediately swept into an embrace for a second time. After a delightful few minutes, he released her. 'A few months ago I was a miserable cripple hiding away in my home. Now look at me. I'm affianced to the most beautiful woman in the kingdom and have four wonderful children in my family.'

'What about this Mr Castleford? Can he still remove the children from our care?'

'Absolutely not. Digby will have the legal papers soon, and then they become my wards.'

'Please don't apply for a special licence, I would much prefer to be married in your church with the children present. If the banns are called as soon as we return, we will only have to wait three weeks. I shall remain at the Dower House for the interim as planned, and that way we will not be tempted to do anything we shouldn't.'

'You will do no such thing — you are moving in with me, and I'll not be gainsaid on this.'

There was a steely look in his eyes, so she decided to accept his dictum, and pray they would not be tempted to pre-empt their wedding night.

The following morning, her dearest Everett accompanied her to see Mr Carberry. The contract was signed, and her first novel would be published in three volumes the following spring. The *nom de plume* she had decided upon was 'Miss Ellen Bell'.

On the way back to Grosvenor Square, they sat together on the squabs. 'You could have used your own name, sweetheart, I would not have minded.'

'I know you wouldn't, which is why I chose not to. I hope you will still be as accommodating once we are wed, my love, as I have a second book to complete before next summer.'

'I have yet to read your first one. Will you allow me to read the one you are writing now?'

She smiled. 'You will find that the hero bears a strong resemblance to yourself, and the heroine to me.'

'Then I am even more determined to read it. Will you have time to prepare your bride clothes in three weeks?'

'Good heavens, I need no new clothes. There is no obstacle to our nuptials, my love, apart from the banns being read.'

She snuggled down against his shoulder, and his arm tightened around her waist. 'Where do you want to go for your bride trip, darling?'

'Nowhere, anywhere . . . I don't care as long as we are together for every single minute.'

He lowered his head so his warm breath tickled her ear, and whispered, 'As I intend to keep you in my bed both day and night making love to you, then it matters not to me where we are.'

She sat up so sharply the top of her head hit his chin, causing him to bite his tongue and turn the air blue with his foul language.

'I refuse to remain in bed doing *that* in the same house as my nieces and nephews! We must go somewhere else for our honeymoon.'

He wiped the blood from his mouth and smiled ruefully. 'Then we shall go to a small estate I have in Kent; it's near the sea, and quite isolated. We will not be observed or disturbed there.'

The carriage rolled to a smooth halt

outside the house, where two footmen were waiting to lower the steps and open the door. The staff already knew that she was to be the new duchess, and treated her with unnerving deference. This was something she was going to have to become accustomed to.

When she returned to Hemingford Court, it was to discover the move had taken place in her absence. Her belongings had been unpacked in a pretty apartment on the opposite side of the house to her future husband.

The vicar was to read the first banns that Sunday and the wedding breakfast was already being arranged.

After greeting the children and Viola, she joined him on the terrace. 'I am so happy, my love, that I feel as if I might rise from the ground and float away.'

'As am I, my darling. We have both had a miserable time of it over the past few years, but now our time has come.' He drew her down beside him on the padded settle that had been brought out. 'You think you are happy now, sweetheart, but believe me I shall make you even happier once we can share a bed.'

She stretched up and kissed him. 'I shall hold you to that promise.'

* * *

As a gentleman of his word, when their wedding night came, he did not disappoint.

We do hope that you have enjoyed reading this large print book.

Did you know that all of our titles are available for purchase?

We publish a wide range of high quality large print books including:

Romances, Mysteries, Classics
General Fiction
Non Fiction and Westerns

Special interest titles available in large print are:

The Little Oxford Dictionary
Music Book, Song Book
Hymn Book, Service Book

Also available from us courtesy of Oxford University Press:

Young Readers' Dictionary
(large print edition)
Young Readers' Thesaurus
(large print edition)

For further information or a free brochure, please contact us at:

Ulverscroft Large Print Books Ltd.,
The Green, Bradgate Road, Anstey,
Leicester, LE7 7FU, England.
Tel: (00 44) **0116 236 4325**
Fax: (00 44) **0116 234 0205**

Other titles in the
Linford Romance Library:

NOT INTO TEMPTATION

Anne Hewland

Rejected by local landowner Sir George Foxcroft, Hannah Brockley opens a girls' school in the family home to achieve financial security for herself and her sister Margaret. But then one of the older pupils dies in suspicious circumstances. Both the sympathetic Reverend William Woodward and the handsome Dr Shipley were present that night. Will they help Hannah through a perilous spiral of danger and deceit to find the happiness she seeks — or could one of them be implicated in the crime?

FALLING FOR A STAR

Patricia Keyson

Thea loves her job in TV, but hates her boss Hermione. When Thea gets a chance to interview her favourite movie star, Justin Anderson, Hermione is willing to do anything to sabotage the blossoming romance between her underling and the handsome actor. Then Thea gets the chance to stay in Justin's country mansion and do some in-depth research. But is he really as nice as he seems? And will she become just another one of his easy conquests?

THE POTTERY PROJECT

Wendy Kremer

Commissioned to assess the Midland Pottery Company's financial prospects, Craig Baines faces an angry manager — Sharon Vaughan has had no warning of his arrival. The workforce soon accepts their well-meaning visitor, even though they know his findings could result in dismissals. When Craig detects that someone is pinching china and pitches in with Sharon to help solve the crime, she becomes increasingly aware of her attraction to him. But after his report is complete and he's about to leave, has she left it too late to let him know?

A SURPRISE ENGAGEMENT

Pat Posner

Flora can't understand how she let her best friend, Val, persuade her to pretend to be engaged to Val's brother, Bryce Torman, heir to the Torman estate. It's only supposed to convince their Uncle Hector that Bryce is serious about someone other than the singing star, Jilly Joy, he's recently been spotted with. To make matters worse, Flora and Bryce have got on like chalk and cheese since childhood — and yet Flora finds herself enjoying his 'fake' kisses rather more than she ought to . . .

MARRIED TO MEDICINE

Phyllis Mallett

Dr. Linda Shelton lives a quiet life with her mother, who boards medical staff from the nearby hospital. Linda's life revolves around her career — until Dr. Martin Crossley arrives at the hospital and takes a room at Shelton House. It's clear he is attracted to Linda, and eventually she reciprocates — but their budding romance is soon tested. Mrs. Shelton faces a seemingly unsolvable problem — and, when it all comes right, nothing will ever be the same again . . .